Unceasing

The Queen's Alpha Series, Volume 3

W.J. May

Published by Dark Shadow Publishing, 2018.

This is a work of fiction. Similarities to real people, places, or events are entirely coincidental.

UNCEASING

First edition. March 7, 2018.

Written by W.J. May.

Also by W.J. May

Bit-Lit Series
Lost Vampire
Cost of Blood
Price of Death

Blood Red Series
Courage Runs Red
The Night Watch
Marked by Courage
Forever Night

Daughters of Darkness: Victoria's Journey
Victoria
Huntress
Coveted (A Vampire & Paranormal Romance)
Twisted

Hidden Secrets Saga
Seventh Mark - Part 1
Seventh Mark - Part 2
Marked By Destiny

Compelled
Fate's Intervention
Chosen Three
The Hidden Secrets Saga: The Complete Series

Paranormal Huntress Series
Never Look Back
Coven Master
Alpha's Permission

Prophecy Series
Only the Beginning
White Winter
Secrets of Destiny

The Chronicles of Kerrigan
Rae of Hope
Dark Nebula
House of Cards
Royal Tea
Under Fire
End in Sight
Hidden Darkness
Twisted Together
Mark of Fate
Strength & Power
Last One Standing
Rae of Light
The Chronicles of Kerrigan Box Set Books # 1 - 6

The Chronicles of Kerrigan: Gabriel

Living in the Past

Staring at the Future

Present For Today

The Chronicles of Kerrigan Prequel

Question the Darkness

Into the Darkness

Fight the Darkness

Alone in the Darkness

Lost in Darkness

Christmas Before the Magic

The Chronicles of Kerrigan Prequel Series Books #1-3

The Chronicles of Kerrigan Sequel

A Matter of Time

Time Piece

Second Chance

Glitch in Time

Our Time

Precious Time

The Hidden Secrets Saga

Seventh Mark (part 1 & 2)

The Queen's Alpha Series

Eternal

Everlasting
Unceasing
Evermore

The Senseless Series
Radium Halos
Radium Halos - Part 2
Nonsense

Standalone
Shadow of Doubt (Part 1 & 2)
Five Shades of Fantasy
Shadow of Doubt - Part 1
Shadow of Doubt - Part 2
Four and a Half Shades of Fantasy
Dream Fighter
What Creeps in the Night
Forest of the Forbidden
Arcane Forest: A Fantasy Anthology
Ancient Blood of the Vampire and Werewolf

THE QUEEN'S ALPHA SERIES
UNCEASING

USA TODAY BESTSELLING AUTHOR
W. J. MAY

Cover design by: Book Cover by Design

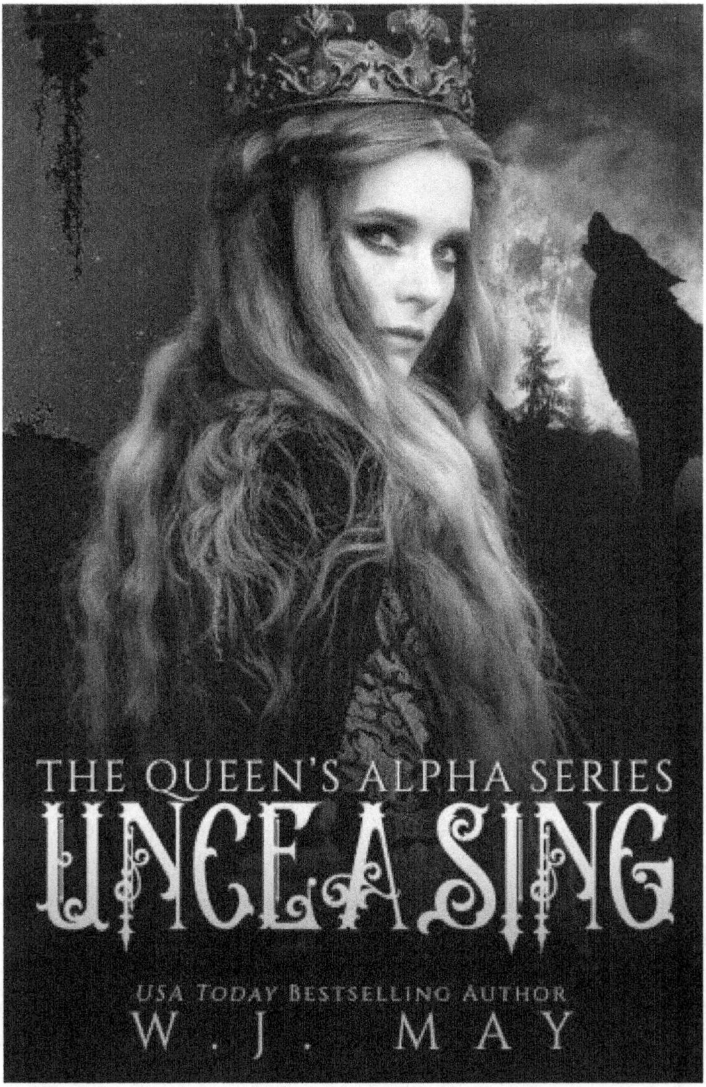
THE QUEEN'S ALPHA SERIES
UNCEASING
USA TODAY BESTSELLING AUTHOR
W.J. MAY

Have You Read the C.o.K Series?

The Chronicles of Kerrigan

Book I - *Rae of Hope* is FREE!

BOOK TRAILER:

http://www.youtube.com/watch?v=gILAwXxx8MU

How hard do you have to shake the family tree to find the truth about the past?

Fifteen year-old Rae Kerrigan never really knew her family's history. Her mother and father died when she was young and it is only when she accepts a scholarship to the prestigious Guilder Boarding School in England that a mysterious family secret is revealed.

Will the sins of the father be the sins of the daughter?

As Rae struggles with new friends, a new school and a star-struck forbidden love, she must also face the ultimate challenge: receive a tattoo on her sixteenth birthday with specific powers that may bind her to an unspeakable darkness. It's up to Rae to undo the dark evil in her family's past and have a ray of hope for her future.

Find W.J. May

Website:
http://www.wanitamay.yolasite.com
Facebook:
https://www.facebook.com/pages/Author-WJ-May-FAN-PAGE/141170442608149
Newsletter:
SIGN UP FOR W.J. May's Newsletter to find out about new releases, updates, cover reveals and even freebies!
http://eepurl.com/97aYf

USA TODAY
BESTSELLING AUTHOR
W.J. MAY
bring fantasy to life...

EVERLASTING Blurb:

She will fight for what is hers.

When their sanctuary suddenly becomes a prison, Katerina and the gang must work together to save not only themselves, but everyone else in the remote, alpine retreat.

Secrets are revealed and new identities are discovered as the princess delves into her past, uncovering things she never thought possible. Awakening a hidden power buried within.

The stakes have never been so high, and everyone's a target. Can the princess unlock the ancient magic in time? Can they find a way off the mountain before disaster strikes? Most importantly, in a world where everyone's out to get them...

...Who can they trust?

Be careful who you trust. Even the devil was once an angel.

The Queen's Alpha Series

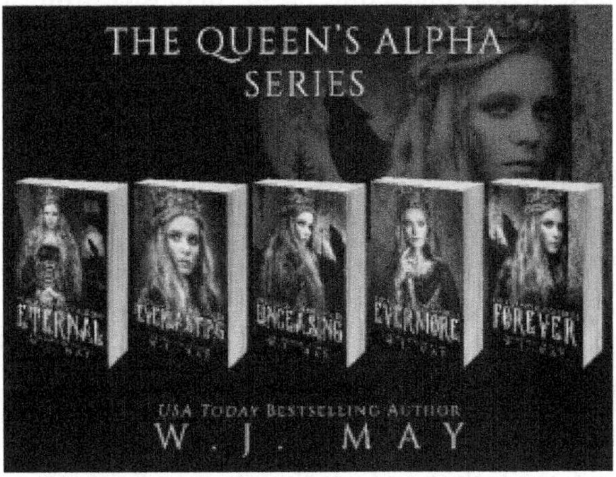

Eternal
Everlasting
Unceasing
Evermore
Forever

Chapter 1

When you've spent so much time racing forward, it's difficult when you finally come to a stop.

Katerina felt as though she was standing on the side of a road, watching a carriage fly by. A part of her was still lurching forward with belated momentum, though her body had long since gone still. Her crimson hair whipped out in front of her, as if caught in a sudden backdraft of wind, but she wasn't moving. None of them were. Their endless journey had finally come to a close.

"Come on!"

A loud banging startled her back to the present. Followed by the soft panting of breath. A searing pain shot through her skull as she opened her eyes, gazing weakly at the world around her.

It was a world of dazzling and deadly extremes. Cliffs that dropped thousands of feet into a swirling sea of mist, and alpine peaks that stretched up to touch the very sky. The stars that had guided them through the long and terrifying night had given way to the lighter hints of dawn. But while the sun had finally risen above the mountains, it was trapped behind an impenetrable layer of clouds—painting the entire picture a surreal shade of white. A color that was pinpricked by a hazy swarm of red and black. The uniform of the royal army, standing just on the other side of the cliff.

Waiting.

Katerina's knees curled into her chest and she leaned as far as she could into the rock behind her. Her head was spinning, overwhelmed by the elevation alone, and as she sucked in a breath of the thin mountain air, gazing out across the abyss, she was reminded of a simple yet terrifying truth.

The journey might be over. But the nightmare had just begun.

"Come on!"

The same voice that had awakened her echoed suddenly louder, and she tilted back her chin to see Cassiel pounding fiercely upon the door that barred the four of them from the sanctuary. His whitened knuckles were smeared with blood, and already there was a small dent in the iron from where his fist was making contact. The noise was deafening. But still, nothing happened.

"Cass?"

He looked down in surprise, and she suddenly realized that the two of them were the only ones still conscious. Tanya was passed out against the door, her hands clutched weakly around the arrow sticking out of her side, and Dylan was lying in a pool of blood beside her. His impossible burst of strength—ripping the blade from his leg and using it to save their lives—had lasted only as long as it needed to, leaving him completely bereft in its wake. His skin was pale white, his chest was barely moving, and despite the belt strapped around his leg that pool of blood was getting bigger.

"Cass, they're bleeding out!"

Why didn't he see it? Why wasn't he doing something?

She pushed shakily onto her palms, but before she could ask either question there was a sudden clattering upon the stone. The mist swirled and her eyes widened as a rogue arrow skidded to a stop at her feet. Just a foot away from where she'd been sitting.

For a second, she simply stared. Turning it over with the point of her shoe. Then she lifted her gaze in terror to the army on the other side of the cliff.

It was only then she understood the frantic pounding. The desperation to get inside. What did it matter if they were bleeding out if they were all about to be killed anyway?

"Oh...right."

The beautiful fae didn't say a thing. He simply looked at her, looked back at the army, then lifted his hands once more to the door. Striking it hard enough to shatter away bits of stone. A second later, she was standing beside him. Pounding against it with all her might.

Ducks in a barrel.

The words came back to her again and again. Like a dark mantra she was unable to shake.

Several years ago, she and a few of her favorite ladies rode out into the forest to meet up with the royal hunt. While women were not allowed to participate directly in such activities, they were permitted to observe and cheer for their favorite knights. When the men got tired of the bloodshed and slaughter, they would retire upon picnic blankets and regale the ladies with stories of their cunning and bravery over pastries and wine. (This had all seemed rather impressive at the time. In light of present circumstances, Katerina couldn't imagine anything more absurd.) At any rate, when they'd finally caught up with the hunt, they were surprised to see not a single animal had been slain.

"What happened?" Katerina remembered asking. "You couldn't find anything?"

Her horse shied back a step to make way for Kailas' powerful steed.

"Oh, we found them all right." His eyes lit up with a dark sort of excitement as he peered down into the trees. "Ducks in a barrel."

The princess followed his gaze with a frown, only to pull back in sudden shock.

An entire herd of snow-white deer was trapped in the ravine down below. While they had clearly fled in terror, the second they were through the bottleneck a large boulder had been rolled forward to seal off any escape. They were still standing there now. Clustered close together. Pawing at the ground in heartbreaking panic. Their lovely eyes wide with fear.

It wasn't until the archers stepped forward that Katerina realized what was about to happen.

"Wait! You can't!" When her brother turned to her coldly, she tried to appeal to his sense of honor. "Where's the sport in that?" she reasoned. "They're completely defenseless. You've won."

Her mistake had been in thinking that there was a sense of honor to appeal to. Kailas didn't have one. He hadn't for a very long time.

"Yes, I have." His lips curled into a wicked smile, and his eyes glowed with anticipation as he slowly lifted his hand. "And now I reap the spoils."

It was a massacre. The sounds of which still haunted her to this day. Katerina didn't go hunting with them after that. And she never rode through that part of the forest again.

That's what we are now. Ducks in a barrel. Trapped on a cliff with nowhere to run and no place to hide.

The bulk of the royal army had endured the same midnight sprint as she and her friends, but it was only a matter of time before the most skilled archers were brought to the front. They were lucky it hadn't happened already. At most, they only had a few more minutes—

A sharp cry echoed suddenly off the rocks.

...or less?

Katerina whipped around to see Cassiel's hand freeze upon the door. At first, it looked as though he'd simply stopped knocking. Then she saw the arrow stabbed straight through his center.

"CASS!"

She raced forward with a shriek as he bowed his head in pain. Tangled strands of blood-soaked hair brushed against his arm as he took a moment to get his ragged breathing under control.

On the other side of the cliff, the archers reloaded with a uniform shout.

"Cassiel, what can I—"

He held up a finger for silence, bracing his body against the wall. A ribbon of blood trickled down his arm, and his eyes were bright with pain. Then, with a strength and resilience the princess would never understand, he took a deep breath, gritted his teeth, and ripped the shaft right out of his flesh.

Holy bloody smokes!

The princess froze in place, mouth agape, staring with unblinking eyes at the bloody handprint stained upon the door. She was still standing there when he reached up and continued knocking with his other fist. It was a fluid transition that barely missed a beat. He only paused long enough to drop the arrow, then grab her cloak and yank her out of the line of fire.

"Keep your head down," he commanded, using his own body as a shield as another volley smashed into the stone just above them, "and keep knocking."

She stared up at him in a daze, like someone trapped in a bad dream. Her body was pinned snugly between him and the door—so close it was hard to breathe. So close she could see every drop of blood clinging to his eyelashes. So close there was only enough room to follow his request.

But while the request might save her, it left him wide open to attack.

"Cass, I can't—" she objected.

She tried to shift away, but he grabbed a fist of her hair and dragged her back again, shoving her roughly against the wall. Their faces were just inches apart as he towered over her. As dazzling as he was terrifying. Making her feel as protected as she was afraid.

"Do as I say."

Their eyes met for a fleeting moment, then she turned around.

Her mind was reeling in horror. Her face was wet with the blood dripping down from his hand. She felt his rapid heartbeat pressed between her shoulders. Felt every ragged, shallow breath whisper across her neck. His muscles tensed with each pounding impact, and at any moment she expected another arrow to sink into his skin. For the warmth of his body to disappear as he fell to his knees. For her last protector in the world to crumble to the ground.

But he didn't. And as long as that was true, they still had a chance.

She pulled in a huge gulp of air and did as she was instructed, pinned between his body and the door. Knocking against the iron with all her might. Teeth rattling with the vibrations as he did the same. Flailing both fists with blinding speed as their cries for help echoed high into the clouds.

There was a quiet moan beside her. So soft she could barely hear. Without breaking her rhythm, she saw Dylan stirring weakly upon the ground. His enchanting face tight with unbearable pain. A faint trembling creeping up his bloodied limbs, even in his sleep.

He doesn't have much time left. None of us does.

Impossible as it was, she began striking the door even harder. Pounding against it with every bit of strength she had left. Summoning up every last reserve. Hitting it so hard that...

...that a spark flew off the metal?

With a quiet gasp she jerked back, staring down at her hands in alarm. Above her, Cassiel continued the desperate assault, oblivious to what had just happened.

Did I just see that right? Her eyes grew wide as saucers as she turned her palms up and down incredulously, searching for any lingering clue. *Could that have possibly been real?*

"Cass..." she began in a trembling voice, "there's something—"

But before she could finish that sentence, there was a metallic groan from somewhere deep inside the mountain. Both she and Cassiel leapt back, dragging their fallen friends with them, as the door they'd been battling so furiously creaked open, revealing a tiny man in a simple brown robe.

It was strangely anti-climactic.

For a moment, both parties simply stared at each other. One side, breathless and exhausted; the other, frozen in shock. Even the arrows came to a stop as everyone gathered held their breath.

Please...please don't turn us away...

The monk's eyes travelled slowly over the bloody teens, then to the army on the other alpine peak, then down into the shadowy abyss that lay between. They lingered there for a moment before coming to rest on the empty wooden posts that once held the bridge that led in and out of the sanctuary. Posts that were still sporting frayed ribbons of rope, blowing gently in the breeze.

At that point the fae stepped back while the princess took a step forward, grimacing apologetically all the while.

"Yeah, it was like that when we got here."

THE NEXT FEW MINUTES passed by in a blur.

There were too many people, too much shouting, and too sudden a swarm of movement for the princess' wearied mind to keep track. The most she could do was keep her eyes open and remain standing as she and the others were carried into the sanctuary. Rather, some of them were carried.

Cassiel had insisted on taking Tanya himself. Wave after wave of blood poured down his shoulder as he knelt with tender care and slipped his hands under her lifeless body. Her tiny arms wrapped around his neck as she was lifted into the air, but her eyes remained shut.

True to form, Dylan had jerked awake the second the first stranger touched him but, try as he might to make sense of the situation, he looked just as lost as Katerina. At first, he staunchly refused the efforts of anyone else to assist him. It wasn't until his mangled leg literally gave out beneath him that he finally accepted a helping hand.

As for the princess, she was simply in shock.

She and the others had been racing on nothing but fumes since their midnight meeting with Alwyn by the pond. Pushing their battered bodies as far as they were physically able to go. Living from moment to moment, painfully aware that each one might be their last.

Now that the chase was over and the world around them had slowed to a stop, that endless night was beginning to catch up with them.

Tanya was placed directly into the hands of a doctor, whisked away in a cloud of antiseptic and gauze. Cassiel—who was still sporting at least five cracked ribs that had never gotten a chance to heal—stopped suddenly in his tracks, coughed up a mouthful of blood, then half-collapsed into the stone wall. He was unconscious before he hit the ground.

Only Dylan remained standing. But he did so only because Katerina was no longer able to stand herself. The second she started to falter, he ripped free of the people trying to hold him and rushed across the damp courtyard, catching her delicately in his arms.

And just like that—all was well.

It didn't matter what the two of them had been through, it didn't matter how they'd left things that night in the woods. They were together now. And they were safe.

Everything else would work itself out in time.

"I thought we were going to lose you." She pressed her face into his jacket and closed her eyes, pulling in a deep breath of that familiar scent. "I thought maybe we'd lost you already."

His arms tightened and he shifted her away from his bad leg. One hand came up to stroke the back of her hair as the other held her tight against his chest. Steady and secure. "I'm not so easy to lose..."

A tired smile pulled at the corner of her lips, and she lifted her head to see him staring down with a twinkling grin. The same grin he'd had the night they met. The one that had kept her strong, kept her sane. The one that had kept her safe and smiling every night since.

But the night was over now. It was time to face the day.

They tried their best to stay together. Tried not to let this bunch of well-meaning strangers separate them. But it was hard enough just to stay awake. The world around them blurred as Tanya vanished in one direction and Cassiel was taken in another. A second later two pairs of strong hands slid in between Katerina and Dylan, prying the two of them gently apart.

"It's okay," a soothing voice murmured, sweeping her legs out from under her. "You're safe now. You can let go."

A few steps away, another cluster of men in brown robes was having a slightly harder time subduing Dylan. The word 'infirmary' was used several times. As well as the coaxing threat of, 'she needs to see a doctor.' It was followed by a much quieter, '...so do you.'

"You can let go," the voice told her again. She lifted her head in a daze, to see a pair of bright blue eyes. Eyes that shone with gentle reassurance. "I promise, it's all right. Just let go."

Let go? Was she still holding on?

She unclenched her fingers at the same time she was whisked away down a stone corridor, flanked between two other tall men. The last thing she remembered was the feel of Dylan's hand as it was ripped away from hers. The look in his eyes as the two of them were torn apart.

Then everything went black.

KATERINA WOKE THE NEXT morning feeling better than she had in ages. She also woke up thinking there was a good chance she had slept for more than just one day.

Her wounds were too healed. The bruises had already begun to fade. And although she felt well-rested she was overwhelmingly weak, as though she hadn't eaten in ages.

The second her eyes adjusted to the light, she pushed shakily to her feet and looked around the room. It was everything the mind conjured when it heard the word 'monastery.' Cold stone floors. Simple twin cot. A roughly-hewn dresser, only large enough to house a few changes of clothes, and a small nightstand pushed up against the window.

No flags. Which she thought was a bit strange. There wasn't a building in the five kingdoms that wasn't required to wave the king's banner. Even the tavern she'd stopped in that first night had one propped up behind the bar. But, on second thought, it was to be expected.

The monks of Talsing Sanctuary belonged to their own order. In effect, the monastery was its own sovereign state. Concepts like kingdoms and political loyalties had no place here. These men had devoted themselves to a higher power. Within these walls, there was no greater authority.

Katerina took inexplicable comfort in that fact as she made her way over to the nightstand.

A brass plate had been placed in the center, complete with a piece of unbuttered toast and several slices of fruit. Beside the plate sat a small cup of water.

She reached out eagerly, then suddenly froze. Too scared to touch it.

What if it had been poisoned? Laid out as some kind of trap? She didn't know these people. For all she knew, she'd been unconscious for days and the army had already found a way inside.

For a second, she was too scared to touch it. Then she was too hungry not to.

The paltry meal only lasted a few moments as the starving princess wolfed it down. The bread was gone in four seconds flat, and the fruit remained a delightful mystery. It didn't look or taste like anything Katerina had tried before, but she knew she'd crave it as long as she lived.

She tried hard to savor the final bites, soaking up every bit of citrusy sweetness, but it was gone too fast and she sat back on the bed feeling a little sick.

Serves you right, you little glutton. Bet the others didn't inhale theirs quite so quickly.

Blinking heavily against the fatigue, her eyes lifted to the window. Outside, the birds were singing. People were bustling cheerfully about on their morning rounds. Even the sun had escaped its misty cage to make a rare, uplifting appearance.

Katerina blinked once. Feeling slightly betrayed.

How is that possible? After everything that's happened? After everything I've seen? How is it possible that the rest of the world is carrying on as though things are somehow okay?

She stared through the glass another moment, lingering on a pair of chattering monks with baskets draped over their arms. Then a far more important question flashed through her tired brain.

Where are my friends?

With the caution of someone who'd spent the last month and a half on the run, she slipped silently out the door and ghosted down the narrow hall. Eyes darting in every direction. Walking on tiptoes, she quickly realized there wasn't a need.

She was completely alone and unsupervised. Free to come and go as she pleased. And while she passed the occasional person in the corridor, they flashed polite smiles but paid her no mind.

It made her feel a lot better about eating the food.

After a few minutes, she finally made it through the maze of stone corridors and into the outside world. It may have been sunny, but the elevation made it a lot colder than it had looked from back in her room. Cold enough that she reached automatically to tighten her travelling cloak.

It was only then she realized she was wearing a simple white cotton dress. The same kind of thing she'd seen on maids back at the castle. The same kind of thing she saw on the other rare women mixed amongst the men milling about the courtyard.

Shouldn't someone be talking to me? She came to an uneasy stop in the middle of the cool grey stones, peering nervously around her. *Shouldn't we be discussing the fact that the royal army is waiting outside?*

She froze uncertainly, giving people the chance to approach her if they should wish, before her eyes latched onto a familiar head of hair. Two of them, in fact. White-blonde and cinnamon.

With a sigh of relief, she hurried up the steps to join them on the parapet. A strategic location to be sure. High enough to set them away from the rest of the general population, but central enough that they were still able to see everything going on.

Looks like I'm not the only one who's nervous to be here.

"Hey," she greeted, sliding automatically into line beside them, "when did you guys get up?"

From the looks of things, they had been out there a while. Tanya was sitting in a chair with her leg propped up in a sling. She had that same depleted look about her that Katerina was feeling herself, but was strangely calm at the same time. Cassiel stood beside her. Arms folded lightly across his chest. Staring silently over the high stone wall at the rows of battalions just beyond.

Jumping slightly, as if she hadn't seen the princess coming, Tanya flashed her a quick smile.

"Yesterday afternoon. Apparently, I spent the first two nights in the infirmary under some kind of sedation, but finally came 'round." She cocked her head towards the fae. "This one and his demented twin were already awake, terrorizing the medical staff. You're the last one."

The first two nights? So I was right. We've been here a while.

Katerina's first reaction was to be deeply disturbed that they'd been sedated without any sort of permission, but just one look at her friends told her that it was the right thing to do.

She couldn't remember the last time Tanya had a spot of color in her cheeks. The last time that Cassiel could pull in a full breath without a shooting stab of pain. The bloody bandage on his hand was brand new, but so was the injury that caused it. An injury she remembered in sudden, perfect clarity as she flashed back to their time together on the cliff.

"...Cass?"

In truth, she didn't know what to say. Where did one begin? With a simple thank-you? After the risk he'd taken, literally holding his body over hers? It seemed too small a gesture.

His eyes flashed over, and for a suspended moment both he and the princess locked eyes. A moment was all that it took. She should have known he wasn't one to dwell.

Instead, he flashed a brisk smile and cocked his head towards the wall. "Dylan will want to know you're awake."

She blinked a second, struggling to change course, then followed his gaze up a tiny winding staircase that led to the roof. Even from where she stood, she could see the corner of a familiar cloak blowing in the breeze. The heel of a boot dangling carelessly in the air.

Of course, the bloody ranger has to pick the tallest mountain in the world, then climb to the very top of it. Of course, he can't keep his feet firmly planted on the ground. The man is deranged.

"That looks...safe."

Tanya flashed a grin, but Cassiel merely returned his eyes to the cliff.

"He spends all his time there." A faint smile ghosted across his face. "Well, either there or sitting beside your bed."

A furious blush spread across her cheeks, and she found herself glad no one was looking.

"Yes, well, that's his job," she said rather lamely. When this got no response, she was quick to add, "I'm actually paying him, you know." *I didn't give up my mother's pendant for nothing.*

The fae merely rolled his eyes, while Tanya shot her a sideways grin. "Uh-huh."

Sensing it was probably best if she made a discreet exit, the princess waved an awkward hand then scampered up the winding staircase Cassiel had pointed to. Each stone step was smaller and more uneven than the last, and by the time she reached the top she was literally clinging to the walls on both sides just for balance.

"You sure this is high enough?" she called out in a teasing voice that did little to hide her anxiety. "Maybe there's a weather vane or something you can nest upon."

She didn't even hear him move, but the next second there he was. Standing framed in the doorway. His dark hair blowing gently into his eyes. His hands at the ready, reaching out to hers.

"You're awake," he said in surprise. Then he was quick to grab her. "Kat, what are you doing up here—you're going to fall."

Her foot slipped on the tile beneath her, but she defiantly held her ground.

"Why do you automatically assume that?" Her fingers dug into the sides of his cloak, hanging on for dear life. "You know, contrary to public opinion, I'm actually not a klutz."

His eyes twinkled as a dozen or more memories to the contrary flashed through his mind, but he kept them to himself. Gently guiding her to a seat beside him on the smooth stone.

"How are you feeling?" he asked instead.

She settled down beside him, trying hard to objectively consider the question. There was a way to come at it from most every side.

Physically: not all that bad. A little weak. A little dizzy. But not all that bad.

Mentally: still trying to catch up. Confused. Disoriented. Waiting for the dust to settle.

Emotionally: probably best not to even touch that one.

"I'm fine," she replied with a quick smile. "What about you?"

His eyes twinkled again as the obvious lie hung in the air between them. It was a casual dismissal. One she'd learned from him. One she wasn't able to pull off nearly as well.

"I'm fine, too."

Shocker.

This time they were unable to keep from laughing. It burst out of them with no warning, soft and sudden. More indicative of damage than mirth, but at this point they were both glad to simply have the option. After the other night, things could have gone the other way.

"I see the army still hasn't moved," she said quietly, the second they'd finally stopped.

For a moment, she almost regretted saying anything at all. Every bit of laughter faded from his eyes as he gazed out across the swirling sea of clouds that separated them. As poorly as her eyes could make out the splashes of color, the red and black dots of the royal uniform, he was able to see them a hundred times better. Picking out individual faces. Picking out individual blades.

"Why would they?" There wasn't a trace of emotion left in his voice. It was simply flat. "For the first time, they know exactly where you are. And they know you're not going anywhere."

A bit of strain crept in at the end, and she peered sideways through her curtain of hair to study him. The look on his face was the same as the others. Subdued. Quiet. Eerily calm. But at the same time there was a hint of dread.

At first, she had attributed this to the aftershock of the chase. Those hours between midnight and dawn weren't something you could shake through sheer force of will. And as if the physical damage wasn't bad enough, there were also the psychological ramifications to consider. The debilitating flashbacks, punctuated with the silent echoes of their screams.

But as the morning began to inch by, she was coming to understand that the nightmarish chase was only half of it. It was the present that had them worried. It was the future.

After all the weeks of running, after all those close calls and hair-raising evasions, they had finally been caught. Yes, they were still technically safe, but the game was over. The deadly dance had come to an end. They were in a cage now. Staring out through the bars at people who wanted to kill them on all sides. People who were content to wait. People who would show them no mercy.

No, it wasn't something you could shake. And Katerina didn't think for a moment that, as Dylan gazed out across the abyss, he wasn't thinking about the hundreds of lives he'd taken the moment he decided to cut the cables on that bridge.

"I just can't believe we made it," she said quietly, momentarily setting their other problems aside and focusing instead on this one shining truth. "We're alive. The *whole army* was chasing us down, but we're still alive." Her voice grew suddenly shy as her eyes flickered to him again. "And that's all thanks to you."

He glanced over sharply, caught off guard by her rather generous assessment. "Me?" A peculiar look flashed across his face before he shook his head curtly. "I got shot, Kat. I got shot and blacked out. You and Cass were the ones who got us in here."

"I'm talking about before that," she pressed gently. "We wouldn't have even made it to the door. We wouldn't have even had the chance if you hadn't cut—"

"I don't want credit for that."

The conversation ended as quickly as it had begun. Neither side had gained any ground. But a silent understanding had been reached.

After a moment, Dylan glanced over at her again. "At any rate, we're not out of the woods yet."

Katerina's spine stiffened automatically, as she was suddenly aware of the bustling monastery behind her. Of the silent horde of faceless monks.

"No one will talk to me," she said under her breath, glancing over her shoulder as if they might be listening anyway. "When I woke up, I just wandered out here—"

"That's because they're all talking to each other." He ran his fingers through his hair with an air of uncharacteristic resignation. "They're deciding whether or not they'll allow us to stay."

Katerina's mouth fell open, and she blinked in shock.

She hadn't once—not for a single moment—considered that might be a problem. Her mind had focused with such tunnel-vision clarity on simply 'reaching the sanctuary door,' that she had never considered what might happen once they made it inside. She'd gotten assurances from Alwyn that the monks would grant them safe haven. That he'd be sending them a message. But even if he hadn't they were *monks*, right? Surely they wouldn't turn the four of them into the cold.

Not that they could anyway. They're trapped up here now, too, same as the rest of us.

"But...of course they will!" Her voice cracked with a wave of panic. "I mean, won't they? I know they have to be angry about their bridge, but I'm sure there's a way to—"

"I don't know, Kat," Dylan interrupted quietly. There was that strange resignation again. An uncharacteristic surrender from a man accustomed to having everything under control. "I don't know."

The wind picked up, tossing their hair in a little cloud around them as the two fell quiet. For the first time since leaving the tavern together all those weeks ago, the decision at hand wasn't theirs to make. They received only the consequences, none of the control. For the first time since they'd left the tavern, their fate was resting entirely in someone else's hands.

For the first time, Dylan's isolated perch made sense. So did that bleak expression.

"Hey, it's going to be all right." Without stopping to think she slipped her hand into his, giving it a comforting squeeze. "These guys are monks. They're not going to just send us..."

A throat cleared suddenly behind them.

"...on our way."

The two of them looked around to see a young man in a brown robe. The same man who'd opened the monastery door. Leather sandals. Corded belt. Hair cropped close to the head.

His eyes swept over them for a moment, taking in every detail, before he gestured down the staircase with a polite smile. "He's ready to see you now."

Dylan pushed to his feet, but Katerina stayed frozen in place—incapacitated by a sudden wave of fear. "Who?"

The monk smiled again, but it was neither comforting nor warm. It was simply a reflex. A conversational filler to get people from one moment to the next.

"You're about to find out."

Chapter 2

The monks of the Talsing Sanctuary might have been ignoring them before, going about their daily chores as if nothing out of the ordinary had happened, but the second the four friends were summoned to the 'meeting room,' all of that changed.

It was as though a curtain had been pulled back. Revealing them for the first time.

Katerina stuck close to the others as they were shepherded down one flight of stairs and then up another. Lost in a series of identical stone hallways, each more circuitous than the last. She ignored the probing eyes and muffled whispers, ignored the pointing fingers and the way a hundred different pairs of eyes lit up with scarcely-contained enthusiasm. She kept her head down and her eyes fixed always on the step right in front of her. Comforted that Dylan was standing by her side.

I wonder if they know who I am, she thought absentmindedly as they wound their way through another endless series of halls. *I wonder if they've guessed that I'm the missing princess.*

It wasn't too far of a stretch. By now, the entire countryside had been plastered with Kailas' damn wanted posters, and one would have to have been living underwater to have escaped the news that the king had died. Then there was always the fact that the royal army was parked right outside.

But, on second thought, Katerina wasn't so sure. The lack of imperial flags and banners was only the beginning. These people were completely isolated. Living at the very top of the tallest mountain in all of the five kingdoms. If there was a solitary place on earth that wasn't at all concerned with the political death games circling the head of Katerina Damaris, this might be it.

To be honest, it was an almost absurd kind of relief. One that broke through the weighty matters at hand, and tickled Katerina with the novelty as she realized that her three friends were getting just as many stares and whispers as she was.

But the monks weren't the only ones doing the staring.

"I thought this was some kind of church," Tanya whispered, one arm wrapped around Cassiel for support as she limped along, trying to keep pace. "I thought everyone here was a monk."

So had Katerina. But, clearly, there was more to Talsing Sanctuary than met the eye.

While it had initially been hard to see anything past the sea of brown robes, it was becoming clear that the monks of the order were only part of the general population. For that matter, they didn't even necessarily seem to be in the majority. The people who lined the halls, stretching up on their tiptoes for a glimpse of the mysterious travelers, would have looked more at home in Vale than they did living at the top of a mountain.

There were creatures and people of all shapes and sizes. At every age and walk of life. From human-looking children to clusters of pixies, to a towering troll who looked so solemn it was all Katerina could do to avert her eyes. It was more of a village than a strict religious order. A village so surprisingly diverse the princess didn't know how she hadn't spotted it immediately.

Maybe they were all hiding from the army, she thought suddenly, her eyes flickering from one supernatural face to the next. *Maybe they were all trying to keep out of sight until we proved not to be a threat.*

Whatever the hesitation, it was gone now. At one point, a tall group of men actually tripped over themselves in an effort to open the final door before Katerina had to do it herself. She and Dylan stepped back in surprise, and as the tallest of them slipped and fell to the floor a sudden giggle of laughter echoed from somewhere back down the hall.

Katerina glanced over her shoulder in time to see a young woman standing behind them in the tunnel, shaking her head with a sarcastic smile. Her eyes sparkled strangely in the dim light, dancing with a wry grin, before they flickered over the clumsy men and came to rest on the princess.

For a second the two women shared a silent look. A silent look paired with a curious frown. Then Katerina and her friends were whisked away and the woman vanished into the crowd.

"Don't say a thing," Dylan murmured under his breath as the gang passed beneath a tall stone archway. "Let me do all the talking."

Katerina was more than happy to oblige. The 'meeting room' might not have been as austere or intimidating as the great judgement halls of the castle, but there was an undeniable weight to it. A sense of gravity that made her straighten up with a little shiver.

And that must be 'him.'

There, sitting in the center of it, was a man who looked as old as time. He didn't have all the trappings—there was no tumbling white beard, no sea of ancient wrinkles to obscure the knowing eyes. Quite the contrary. He was fit and stately and didn't look older than fifty.

But there was something about him all the same.

This man had been alive longer than anyone she'd ever met. Katerina was suddenly sure of it. He'd seen things, and experienced things, and done things the rest of them could only dream of.

Already, Cassiel was looking at him like a kindred spirit.

He waited patiently until the room had filled to capacity, letting the people of Talsing cram inside, then raised a hand for silence. The order was immediately followed, and a sudden hush swept over the entire room. It was then that he stood, staring intently at his unexpected guests.

"Before anything else, I'm incredibly pleased to see you all back on your feet." His voice was quiet, too. Not that it mattered. The room was hanging on every word. "It looks as though none of you sustained any permanent injuries. For that we can be glad."

It was a kind way to break the ice, and all at once Katerina felt a rush of gratitude for the days of sedation. There was a fleeting pause, then Cassiel stepped forward with a gracious smile.

"That is thanks entirely to you." He was as charming as he was sincere. A far cry from the fearsome warrior Katerina had seen on the cliff. Yet, between the two of them, it was suddenly easy to see the High Born prince that lay dormant inside. "You have our eternal gratitude—not only for opening your doors, but for the care we received once we were inside. We thank you. Truly."

At that point, both Katerina and Tanya stepped quickly forward with murmured words of gratitude. Only Dylan stayed where he was. Keeping his eyes locked on the floor.

Okay, so when he said 'let me do all the talking,' I take it he meant Cassiel instead?

It was true. The fae glanced quickly behind him, his eyes flickering almost imperceptibly to the ranger's face. They rested there for a brief moment as a silent communication was exchanged. A second later he turned back to the front, and it was as if the entire thing never happened.

"Allow us also to apologize," he continued quietly, "for the circumstances of our arrival."

'Circumstances of our arrival.' That was a generous way of putting it. The lovely fae was so composed and disarming, that for a moment it was almost easy to forget that he and his friends had destroyed a centuries- old bridge. Essentially imprisoning every monk and villager inside.

The man in charge seemed to think so, too. His eyebrows lifted with the hint of a smile, and for a second Katerina could have sworn he looked right at Dylan. Then he returned to the fae.

"Let us not mince words. We have no allegiance to the royal army that followed you here, neither do we wish them any harm. The Talsing Sanctuary is above political entanglements. An order and authority all to itself. As such, we will not involve ourselves either way."

The princess stifled another shiver and moved closer to her friends. They wouldn't involve themselves? Did that imply a certain unwillingness to harbor political refugees?

Cassiel's eyes flickered up uncertainly, but before he could say a word the man continued.

"Neither do we have any intention of turning you into the cold. For over a thousand years, the sanctuary has opened its doors to anyone in need of guidance. They need only ask."

For the second time, the man's eyes came to rest upon Dylan. They lingered there for a moment, softening with an emotion Katerina didn't understand, before he reached into his pocket and pulled out a single piece of paper scrawled hastily in a looping hand.

"Furthermore, someone has seen fit to ask for you." The paper fell open, though it was too far away for anyone to read. "Only moments before your arrival, I received a message from an old acquaintance requesting safe haven for you and your friends. This haven will be granted for as long as it's necessary. You have nothing to fear from the people inside these walls."

Again, Katerina was overwhelmed with a rush of gratitude. At the same time, she found herself overwhelmed with questions and tried to think back to anything and everything she could remember from the brief conversation between the wizard and the ranger at the pond.

When Alwyn had suggested Talsing, Dylan had been doubtful. More than doubtful, he'd flat out questioned the wisdom of such a proposition.

"*If* the monks grant her safe passage," he'd countered. "And why would they? She's not a student; it isn't a safe house for wayward royalty—"

The word lodged in her brain, and she looked around with sudden curiosity. A student? Was this place some kind of school? And the man in charge...he was like the headmaster?

"Well...thank you," Cassiel said softly, blinking at the floor in surprise. He had obviously counted on going several rounds with this intimidating man, trying to ensure a place for them within the walls. He hadn't expected it to be offered on a silver platter. "That's incredibly kind."

Again, his eyes flickered back to Dylan. This time they seemed to be prompting. Urging him to step forward as well. But the ranger stayed frozen in place, his gaze fixed firmly upon the floor.

"Of course, now that the bridge has fallen, we'll have to discuss what steps to take." For the first time, the man's voice rose a bit sharply. "Our provisions are supplemented from the villages at the base of the mountains. There's only so long we can subsist on what's already inside."

"We will!" Katerina blurted before she could stop herself, staring up at the man with tears of apology shining in her eyes. "We're so sorry for putting you at any sort of risk. I can never tell you just how sorry. We'll make it right. I promise."

Cassiel tensed, Tanya paled, and Dylan glanced up for the first time. All unsure about such an honest admission of guilt. But the man was looking down at her with a spark of interest. As if, for the entire audience, he'd been waiting to hear what she had to say.

They don't need banners or flags. This man knows exactly who I am.

Their eyes met for the briefest moment, then he turned away with a smile.

"In that case, I'll advise you all to get some rest. The monks will supply you with anything you need, and we can talk more in the days to come."

Just like that, the meeting was over. It ended as quickly as it had begun. Cassiel and Tanya were still murmuring words of thanks when the man swept suddenly out of the chamber from a door on the side. It wasn't until he was gone that Katerina realized she didn't even know his name.

"That's it?" she whispered to Tanya as the room began to empty out. A few brave people flashed them tentative smiles, while others seemed more eager to discuss the details amongst themselves. "That's all there is to say?"

"It's enough," Cassiel interjected softly. He, too, was watching people file noisily from the room. "Under the circumstances, we couldn't have asked for anything more. Michael's a good man."

"Michael," Katerina repeated in a daze. "Is that his name?"

She glanced automatically back at Dylan, but he was already heading to the door. Winding his way through the mass of people without really looking at anyone. When he got to the edge, he paused and waited for the others.

All of whom looked at him with varying degrees of confusion and exasperation before following him out.

It wasn't until the princess was sweeping past him that he leaned down and caught her arm. "What happened to keeping your mouth shut?" he asked under his breath.

She yanked her arm free, staring up with the hint of a glare. "I'm sorry. I figured you were keeping quiet enough for the both of us."

A wave of guilt flashed across his face, and he opened his mouth to say something, but she was out the door before he could get out a word. Together, the four friends followed the crowd through the winding labyrinth of corridors and back into the outside world.

They were just pouring out into the courtyard, when there was a flash of raven-colored hair and a shadowy figure went barreling right into Dylan's arms.

"Oh, I'm sorry!" The others stepped back in surprise as the young perpetrator righted herself quickly, one hand still wrapped around the ranger's arm. "I didn't see you there."

It was the girl from down in the tunnels, Katerina realized. The same one who had laughed when the men tripped over themselves to help them before.

Up close, she was even more beautiful than the princess had imagined. A slender, athletic frame. Smooth, mocha-colored skin. Long, silky hair. And lips that always seemed to be somewhere between a smirk and a pout. But far and away, the most bewitching thing about her was her eyes.

In her entire life, Katerina had never seen such incredible eyes. One was dark espresso, while the other was electric blue. An almost startling combination, but it fitted the girl like a glove.

She was the kind of girl the men at the castle would have fawned over. The kind that Katerina had always watched with a bit of jealousy from the confines of her chambers.

The hint of a dimple puckered at the corners of her lips as she flashed Dylan a seductive smile. A smile that barely masked the brazen boldness underneath. "I can be so clumsy sometimes."

He made sure she was steady before casually unwrapping her hand. It was a clear dismissal, but Katerina could have sworn he did it with a bit of a grin. "I'll bet."

There seemed to be more to the words than was said. The same way the greeting between the two came off as just the slightest bit strange. The way they leaned towards each other without seeming to think about it. The way they took in every detail, a lingering smile in their eyes.

It set Katerina's teeth on edge.

"I'm Kat." She held out her hand before she could stop herself, surprising everyone standing in the little circle, no one more than herself. Usually, these kinds of women were to be avoided. But this one seemed to require a little confrontation. At least, that's what the princess told herself.

The girl stared at her for a moment before peeling herself away from Dylan as her face lit up with a genuine grin. "Rosaline Macado." They shook briefly. "But everyone here calls me Rose."

I'll bet they do.

The princess' eyes made a rather sullen study of her face as the rest of the friends proceeded to make their own introductions. Realizing, with a heavy heart, that the situation was even worse than she could have imagined.

The girl was *likeable*. Friendly. Playful. Warm. Before Katerina realized what was happening, she was horrified to discover that the lovely woman had actually made her smile.

...bitch.

"—granted, I've only been here about twelve months myself, but in all that time I've never seen anyone new come through the door. And the way you guys did it?" She shook back her long hair, looking distinctly impressed. "Let's just say, they'll be talking about it for a long time to come."

The others shared a silent look, unsure how they felt about that. But before any of them could respond, a bell sounded from high in the clock tower and the girl jumped back to attention. A second later she was tearing across the courtyard, the same as everyone else.

"Anyway, it was nice meeting you!" she called over her shoulder. "I'll see you around."

Katerina and Tanya lifted their hands in a half-hearted wave, but she was already gone. Their fingers wilted as they gazed with wide eyes around the suddenly deserted courtyard instead.

"What the heck just happened?" the shifter demanded. "Should we be getting inside, too?"

Dylan merely shook his head, looking suddenly tired. "They're going in for classes. For classes and prayers. We're free to have this time for ourselves."

Katerina stared at him curiously, but he carefully avoided her eyes.

"Come on," he said, leading them back towards the chambers, "let's get settled in."

They were already halfway across the courtyard before Michael stepped outside.

Almost all the way to the door before he called out softly. His eyes fixed on the back of the ranger's head. "Dylan."

The ranger's shoulders tightened as his skin paled. For a moment, it looked like he was going to turn around. Then he kept on walking as if he hadn't heard the call.

What the heck's going on?

Katerina glanced discreetly over her shoulder, eyes already tight with apology, but the man didn't look surprised. In fact, he was staring back with steady patience.

As if the boy had been walking away from him for a long time.

Chapter 3

That night Katerina lay in bed, not sleeping for hours. Staring up at the ceiling. Thinking over the events of the day. The four friends had spent the afternoon and evening together—having realized that their rooms were next door to each other—and even shared a simple meal on Tanya's bed. But despite having time alone for discussion, there ended up being very little to talk about.

Dylan was lying. That's all there was to it.

He had obviously been here before. The maze of corridors didn't confuse him. He knew where the kitchen staff kept the extra bowls. Prayers started at six. Dinner started at nine. He knew it all. Not to mention the fact that he obviously had some complicated history with Michael.

But Katerina couldn't for the life of her get him to talk about it.

Tanya simply didn't care. As long as the gang was safe on one mountain, with the royal army trapped all the way on another, she seemed content to focus on healing her broken leg and enjoy as many hot meals as she possibly could. Not that Katerina could blame her.

Cassiel obviously knew the truth but didn't care to tell the princess. He and Dylan had an even longer and more complicated history than Dylan and Michael. If the ranger wanted to keep certain things to himself, there was no way that Cassiel was going to break his trust.

Which left Dylan. But the man was a vault.

At countless points during the afternoon and evening Katerina found herself thinking that, if it weren't for his natural born aversion to political bullcrap, he would have made a fine lawyer back at the castle. Never had she witnessed such skillful deflection. So many deft evasions. It wasn't that he ever actually lied, he just simply bent over backwards to avoid the truth. And as long as that was the case, Katerina didn't know if she'd ever find out what was going on.

A sudden knock on the door made her jump. Followed by a whisper in the dark.

"Kat, are you awake?"

Speak of the devil, and he'll come knocking on your door.

Quiet as a mouse, she leapt out of bed and scampered across the floor, wishing she had a robe to wrap around her thin nightgown. How did the monks stand it? It was so cold!

"Listen, stalker," she teased as she pulled open the door, "I've had quite enough of these late-night—" She broke off suddenly as her eyes came to rest not on Dylan, but on the beautiful girl standing beside him. "Oh...hi, Rose. What's... uh... what's going on?"

Dylan opened his mouth to reply, but Rose beat him to it. Her bright eyes twinkled different colors under the torches mounted on the walls.

"We were heading out to get a drink." Her eyes swept Katerina up and down with a little smile. "Wanted to know if you'd like to come along."

The princess' first impulse was to refuse. Not just because she was dressed in nothing but a freezing cold nightgown, while this girl was decked out in a corset and what looked like black leather pants, but also because she didn't want to seem too eager to come. So, Dylan and the little she-devil were headed out for late-night drinks? Why would she volunteer to be a third wheel? Maybe things had changed between the two of them. Maybe there was nothing there. He'd felt things while trying to be her knight in shining armor. Maybe now he didn't feel so... much. He wasn't talking to her, refused to admit things. Maybe what they had was fleeting—gone like the bridge across the mountains.

She swallowed and straightened. That might be the case, but her feelings, whatever they were, hadn't changed. She didn't exactly want Dylan to be left alone with the girl either. Rose seemed nice and all. Just a little too pretty, a little too confident, a little too strong, a little too exciting—wait, was Kat jealous?! *Am I jealous?*

"I'm not sure," she stalled, hedging her bets. "I don't really have anything—"

"To wear?" Rose reached suddenly into the leather satchel strapped around her waist and pulled out Katerina's very own travelling cloak. She tossed it to the princess with a knowing grin. "I figured they must have confiscated your stuff when you first got in here. Managed to pilfer this from the laundry before the lady who works there got back from lunch."

Well, wasn't that...genuinely sweet of you. She smiled. *I can't be jealous. This girl's actually nice.*

Katerina took the cloak with a stifled sigh and managed to flash the annoyingly thoughtful girl a grin in return. "Thanks. Not that these dresses the monks gave us aren't great, but—"

"—but they look like something that belongs in a prison?"

The princess laughed, sliding the cloak over her shoulders. "Yeah. Something like that."

Without another word, Rose gestured down the hall and the three of them set off, pausing to collect Tanya and Cassiel along the way. Where they were going to get this mysterious drink within the walls of a monastery, Katerina had no idea. But as she followed the girl down further into the tunnels, she was quick to realize there was more to the monastery than met the eye.

Before they'd gone more than five minutes underground, Rose ducked off the beaten path and pushed open a tiny door carved directly into the stone. If you weren't looking, you would never have seen it. A door that led to a merry little tavern nestled beneath the foundations of Talsing itself.

"This is incredible," Katerina murmured, staring around with wide eyes at what looked like the world's most exclusive speakeasy. "The monks built all this themselves?"

Rose shook her head, settling down at a table and snapping her fingers for the guy running the bar to bring them some drinks. "Inherited it. Whoever came here before us—they obviously had a lot of time on their hands. And a lot of whiskey and cider."

Whiskey proved to be the key word. Cider as well.

The shots went down easy, and by the time the gang was two or three drinks in the afternoon intrigue was laid to rest. The broken bones were compartmentalized away. Even the army camped on the other side of the ravine was temporarily forgotten. Escapism was the name of the game. And heaven knew, after everything the four friends had been through they'd earned a temporary escape.

Dylan settled back and actually released the handle of his blade, Cassiel and Tanya made eyes at each other from across the table, Katerina finally managed to silence those worried questions flying around her head, and Rose? Rose turned out to be a bit of a delight.

"To dodging arrows." She raised her fourth glass in a jubilant toast, then registered the sardonic faces staring back at her with a little grimace. "Oh. Right. Well, to living through them."

The gang laughed and clinked their glasses against hers, downing them in a single shot.

The four friends had clearly been to hell and back and, curious as she might have been, Rose knew better than to pepper them with questions. But the more of their story had leaked out, the more anecdotes had begun piling up—the more absurd the entire thing had become.

"You know, I honestly don't know which is worse—" she muttered under her breath, eyes flashing two different colors as she tried to imagine it. "The avalanche or the woods."

"The woods," Katerina, Dylan, and Tanya said in unison.

As one, the rest of the table turned and looked at Cassiel.

He paused with his whiskey halfway to his lips, but somehow still managed to project a look of total innocence. "...I didn't think the woods were that bad."

Katerina snorted under her breath, while Dylan slowly raised his eyebrows. Considering that he had nearly been decapitated then hacked to pieces while strangled by roots, he had a slightly different perspective. So did Tanya, for that matter. Though she kept her opinions to herself.

"At any rate, I scarcely remember the woods." The fae set down his glass, acting as though they were all exaggerating a great deal. "The avalanche almost killed us all."

"Not Kat," Tanya said suddenly. She cocked her head curiously to the side, as if she was piecing it together for the first time. "Kat managed to walk away without a scratch."

"That's true," Cassiel backed her up quickly, thrilled to have shifted the conversational blame away from himself. "You were composed enough to stab that dagger between my ribs." Rose lifted her finger with an automatic question, but it was ignored. "And how is that, exactly?"

For the first time since they'd sat down at the table, Katerina shifted a little nervously in the sudden spotlight. It was a question she had asked herself many times. Ever since they'd stumbled away from the scene of the crime. The others had been barely holding it together—broken and battered and buried beneath a mountain of snow. But her? It was as if she'd been tucked away by a pair of velvet gloves. Not a scratch on her body. Not a single hair out of place. She assumed it was because they were all protecting her. Nothing more.

"How is it that I managed to *stab* you?" She tried to deflect the question with a joke. "To be honest, Cass, I'd wanted to do it for a long time, and I figured I'd never get a better chance than when you were already half-dead—"

A grin flashed across his face, but he didn't let it go.

"I'm serious." His eyes grew thoughtful as he played the ghastly day back in his mind. "All of us were caught up in it. All of us were almost killed. But you just walked away..."

It was a question that needed an answer, and three pairs of eyes burned into her face. But, fortunately, the fourth pair saw what the others couldn't. And provided her a gracious escape.

"These crazy fools keep protecting you, don't they?" Rose laughed. "Just lucky, right, Kat?"

She glanced up in relief and saw Dylan watching her with a twinkling smile. At the same time, she remembered their conversation back in the snow. He'd asked her the same question, and she'd given the same reply. He'd let it go then. And was still willing to let it go now.

Her lips curved up in a tentative smile before she shrugged, as casual as could be. "What can I say? Some of us have saved up a little karma. Comes in handy every time there's an avalanche, a rockslide, a flashflood..."

The others laughed and returned to their drinks. Only Rose remained staring at her, eyes dilated with unnatural focus as she tried to figure out the princess' role in the group. What made the others so protective? What made the fragile-looking girl with the bright red hair so important?

Unfortunately for Katerina, it was a game that was best played drunk. And the empty glasses of whiskey had already left the rules of propriety far behind them.

"So, how exactly did you guys all meet up?" Rose began innocently enough. Then the alcohol kicked in and she asked her real question. "And why is the royal army sitting right outside?"

For a moment the little table froze. The rest of the bar quieted just as suddenly, straining their ears to get all the juicy details the sanctuary had been buzzing with since their arrival.

Katerina shot Dylan a look but remained quiet. She had been strangely grateful that the girl had been nothing but good company thus far. That she had kept all those irksome questions to herself. That gratitude was vanishing quickly. As was her own ability to lie.

"Oh, you know those guys," Tanya said with a dismissive scoff. "In the absence of any real problems, they'll jump at the chance to screw somebody. Probably just itching to unionize—"

"It hasn't exactly gotten easier for people of the supernatural persuasion since you came to the sanctuary," Cassiel intervened gracefully. "A band of us travelling together attracted attention."

A brilliant save. But it still begged the obvious question—

"And why were you guys travelling together?" Rose insisted.

The others were uneasy, but she was too drunk to notice it. The tension was so thick you could cut it with a knife, but there was no escape. It had gotten to the point where Katerina thought they would just have to walk away from the table, when Dylan leaned forward with a little smile.

"I'll do you one better...why the heck is there a tavern at the base of a monastery?"

The tension vanished with a burst of laughter. At the same time, a dozen loud conversations started back up all over the bar.

Rose angled Dylan's way with a seductive grin. "The monks know about it, but they've learned to turn a blind eye. There's no harm, and besides, we're not all monks." Her eyes swept him up and down. "Some of us like to play."

That *delightful* girl was vanishing by the minute. Replaced with a drunken little flirt.

"I'm sure you do." Dylan swished the whiskey around in his glass and lowered his eyes to the table. Shutting down every advance before it could begin. The same way he'd been doing all night.

But Rose, it seemed, was unnaturally persistent. In fact, she seemed to rise to the challenge. "So... is it true what they say about rangers?"

Katerina looked up sharply as Dylan slowly lifted his head. On the other side of the table, Tanya shot the princess a quick look before hurrying to intervene.

"What—brooding little narcissists? Giant savior complex?" Tanya downed the rest of her whiskey with a little nod. "Yep. That's rangers all right."

Rose flashed a grin, but kept her eyes locked on Dylan. "How does the saying go? Good with their hands, good with their—"

ENOUGH! "Boys," Katerina waved her glass suddenly in the air, having reached her emotional limit for brazen advances, "why don't you get us all another round? I could use one."

Cassiel lifted his eyebrows with a slight grin but pushed to his feet to do as she'd asked. On his other side, Dylan shot her a glance from the corner of his eye but got up to do the same. It wasn't until they'd vanished to the other side of the room that she turned back to the little hussy, determined to let her have a piece of her mind.

But, again, Rose beat her to the punch. "So, what's the deal with that one?" She cocked her head curiously to the side, following the men with her eyes. Tanya and Katerina followed her gaze before twisting back around, both slightly stiffer than before.

"You mean Dylan?" Katerina asked in a deceptively sweet tone. *Funny you should ask*. "As fate would have it, he's actually—"

"No, not Dylan. The blond."

The girls turned around again in surprise, to see her looking at Cassiel—studying his every move with an almost critical eye. On the other side of the table, Tanya slowly lowered her drink.

Rose, predictably, remained oblivious.

"Doesn't look like much of a warrior," she murmured, looking him up and down. "Too pretty to have ever seen a battlefield. Can the guy even fight?"

Can Cassiel even fight?

Awkward timing aside, it was the perfect thing to say. For the first time all evening, Katerina and Tanya shared a genuine grin. The girl might be unbearably full of herself, but she had missed the mark with that one. Missed it by a mile.

"I don't know—Tanya?" Katerina tilted her head to the side, pursing her lips to restrain an amused smile. "What do you think?"

As if on cue a drunken shifter stumbled towards the bar, spilling his drink in front of Dylan and Cassiel in the process. At first, it looked as though he'd simply fallen. But just a second later, he began spouting off vile profanities and accusing them of bringing a heap of imperial trouble to the sanctuary door. (Not too far off the mark. But boys will be boys.)

At first, they attempted to ignore him. But when he shoved Dylan against the counter, Cassiel apparently decided he'd had enough.

It was over before it had even begun. Over so fast it was hard to keep track of.

One second, the man was advancing with a look of drunken fury. The next, he was lying on his back in a pile of broken glass. Cassiel was standing over him, looking almost bored by the entire proceedings. He hadn't used more than a single arm. He hadn't even spilled a drop from his glass.

"Yeah," Tanya replied with a grin, "I think he can fight."

Rose's mouth fell open as the men returned to the table, each holding a trio of glasses in their hands. For a moment, she simply stared. Then her eyes flickered over to the shifter, who had yet to get to his feet, before she turned back to her friends with a newfound respect. "Wow. You guys should lead the hunting expedition!"

Katerina's eyebrows shot up in surprise, while the men leaned forward with interest.

"Hunting expedition," Cassiel repeated with a frown. "And how exactly is that possible? I thought the only way off this mountain was the bridge that we just...misplaced."

"It may have *technically* been the only path, but we can still get creative." Rose's eyes glittered with anticipation as she looked from one to the other. "That is, if you're willing to take the risk."

A few weeks ago, the gang might have risen to the challenge. That competitive nature was in their blood. Now? They'd taken their share of risks. And they'd been running low on blood.

"Speak plainly," the fae demanded. He had a habit of slipping into a slightly more formal speech when he was annoyed. "Is there another way down or not?"

Rose backed off quickly and was careful to adjust her tone. "Not for an army of mortals, no. But for a few highly talented individuals—yes. There is a way. And, considering the fact that the monastery is going to have to stock up on supplies before long, I think it's a good thing the two of you are here."

The two of them?

Katerina and Tanya glanced at each other at the same time. When Rose had been talking about taking a joint risk, they hadn't imagined for a second that the two of them weren't included.

"Just Dylan and Cass?" Tanya asked innocently. There was a bit of an edge to her voice, one that only her friends were able to recognize. "No one else?"

Rose plowed right on ahead, missing the subtle warning in her words. "Well, I think we all know what you're capable of." She grinned at the ranger before batting her eyes at the fae as well. "And as for you...I've never seen anyone move like that."

At this point Tanya reached over and stole the rest of her drink, while Katerina simply rolled her eyes. A part of her could hardly blame the poor girl. Cassiel looked like some ancient prince. The kind that rescued the princess from the dragon in the tower. As for Dylan?

...Katerina had never met anyone quite like Dylan.

But the girl's constant flirtation didn't bother Katerina nearly as much as what she'd just implied. She remembered the look on Dylan's face when the bridge fell to the ground. She knew he'd sat up on that rooftop, staring down at it ever since.

"What he's capable of?" Kat repeated icily. She and the ranger may not have been seeing eye to eye at the moment, but that didn't mean she wasn't absurdly protective. "If he hadn't cut down that bridge, everyone sitting at this table would be dead right now. Probably everyone in this bar. You really think the royal army would have spared a place full of supernaturals? I don't care if it's technically a sanctuary or not—"

"I wasn't talking about the bridge," Rose said quickly, frowning, as if she'd already forgotten it had fallen. "I was talking about the fact that our pretty little ranger is also a wolf."

For the second time, Katerina sat back in her chair. Absolutely stunned. It had taken her weeks to discover Dylan's magical secret. *Weeks*—and they'd been sleeping in the same tent every night. Spending every waking moment together walking up and down the same trails.

This girl shows up less than twelve hours ago and already has it figured it out?

No. He must have told her.

A feeling of deep, irrational betrayal bubbled up in the princess' stomach as she turned to Dylan with wide eyes. She knew she had no claim to him. She knew she shouldn't care. But only a few nights before, she'd been pressed up against a tree. His hands up her dress and his lips smooshing hers. They'd kissed under the stars, and she'd told him that she loved him.

But he walked away.

And now this.

He caught her staring just as she was looking away. He must have seen the look of hurt and confusion cloud across her face, just as she lowered her eyes to the table.

"Kat," he started, reached out and grabbed her hand without thinking, oblivious to the table full of curious onlookers watching his every move, "it isn't like that—"

"What?" Rose asked innocently. "She didn't know?"

For the first time, he looked at the girl directly. Leveling her with a cold glare. "Of course, she knows. I'm just trying to explain—"

"Explain what?" Katerina asked with a forced smile, trying to play the whole thing off like it couldn't matter less. "Explain why the *three* of you will be going on some hunting expedition while Tanya and I will be left behind? And why? Because I'm just human? No offense, Tanya." She glanced at her shifter friend before looking back at Dylan. "Or explain how this girl somehow knows you're a—"

"She knows I'm a wolf because she's a wolf, too."

That brought the conversation to a sudden halt.

Tanya and Cassiel glanced up with matching looks of surprise. Rose tilted back in her chair with a smug smile and blinked innocently. Okay, not so innocently. Katerina stared across the table with scarcely contained shock.

She'd thought there had been something strange about their greeting, an underlying subtext that the others weren't able to see. She'd thought there had been something sarcastic in the way Dylan had smiled when she went tumbling into him, claiming to have made a clumsy mistake. She'd just never suspected it was because they had each recognized a shared magic within the other.

Well, it's official...they're perfect for each other.

After a few seconds of awkward silence Katerina settled back in her chair, tracing the edge of her empty glass and feeling strangely numb. Dylan shifted uneasily as the others shot him a look, trying to catch her eye, but Rose couldn't have been more pleased with how things had turned out.

"Two wolves and a fae," she summarized, as if it was the most natural thing in the world. "I can't think of anyone else who could make it down the cliff without a trail." Her eyes flickered over the other girls. "Especially considering that you two aren't exactly at your best."

While they may not have been 'at their best,' that didn't mean that both Katerina and Tanya weren't perfectly prepared to kick her smug little ass. Already, Tanya was eyeing the cast around her leg like she was ready to break it off and bludgeon the girl to death.

"At any rate, you don't have to worry about any of that with me," Rose said bluntly. "There are a few of us shifters at the sanctuary. All of us can be ready to go at a moment's notice. All you have to do is say the word, and we'll be there."

"I bet you would," Tanya interjected with a scathing look. "All they have to do is snap their fingers, and you'll come running."

The not-so-subtle implication would have been enough to make anyone blush, but Rose only ever smiled. Turning that smile with full force right onto Dylan Aires. "Trust me...I can keep up."

Chapter 4

"Of all the stupid, insufferable, infuriating little shifters—that girl has got to be the worst!" Katerina was storming back down the torch-lit corridor as fast as her drunken feet would carry her, pausing every now and then to circle back as Tanya limped after her in a cast. "I can't believe she's a flippin' wolf!"

Tanya paused to take a breath, leaning against the wall for support as she kneaded tenderly at her braced leg. "Yeah...you mentioned that several thousand times."

Kat shot her friend a look but didn't really pay attention to what Tanya had said. "At any rate, I guess it explains her stupid multi-colored eye thing." Katerina's mind flashed back with a begrudging sort of admiration before she slapped the wall with her hand. "You know what—*no*! I bet the whole eye thing is fake! Just a colored lens or something she uses for attention."

Tanya pursed her lips and began limping along once more. "Yeah. I'm sure that's it."

"Not that it was fooling *anyone*," the princess continued in a rage, completely oblivious to the fact that she was raging alone. "The whole thing makes her seem ridiculous. *Not* that she needed any help looking ridiculous." She came to a stop in front of her bedroom door, promptly forgot how to open a door, and slid down to the floor instead. "Drunken idiot. Can't even hold her liquor."

It was a testament to the strength of the bond they had formed out in the wild that Tanya didn't say a thing. She simply hitched the princess' arm around her shoulder, heaved her to her feet, and twisted open the door with her other hand. "Yeah, that would be super embarrassing."

Katerina nodded with a self-righteous sniff and stumbled clumsily into her room, tripping over every piece of furniture before coming to a stop in front of her bed. "Why aren't you more ticked off about this? She was looking at Cass, too."

This time, it was the shape-shifter's turn to deflect. She met Katerina's eyes for only a second before tossing back her hair with an unconcerned shrug. "And why would that bother me?"

Katerina surfaced from her drunken haze long enough to shoot her a deeply sarcastic look before wallowing in self-pity once more. "I just don't see what she's doing at the sanctuary to begin with. The girl said it herself: she's no monk..."

She trailed off piteously as Tanya came and perched beside her on the bed.

At the castle, there had been an endless parade of suitors. Not a single day went by that she wasn't inundated with a flood of invitations, and gifts, and marriage proposals. She'd even received the occasional sonnet. But she'd never cared about any of them. Never been attracted. Never once felt that dizzying wave of breathless incapacitation the way she did every time she saw Dylan.

It was *excruciating*. And to be frank, the princess quite simply didn't know what to do. This was unchartered territory here, and she was working without a net. Those two glasses of whiskey she'd had to drink weren't helping matters. Neither were the ones that followed.

Fortunately, at least one good thing had happened since she'd left the castle. She might have made half a kingdom's worth of enemies, but she had also made a friend.

"The girl's a straight-up wench," Tanya declared, leaning back against the window. The princess nodded soundly, and they both stewed in that for a moment before she continued cautiously. "But, no, she's not a monk. She's probably a student. A lot of supernatural kids are sent to sanctuaries like this when they're young by parents who can't protect them. They come here to get an education. They learn to protect themselves."

Katerina mulled this over as well as her whiskey-soaked mind was able. She recalled Dylan saying something about people going to classes as well as going to prayers. Part-tavern, part-school, part-religious order...it was too much to keep track of.

"But that's not the real question." She looked up to see Tanya staring at her with a coaxing smile. "The real question is why you care if she was flirting with Dylan."

Crap! I probably should've seen that one coming. The princess froze with cartoonish guilt, trying to figure out her next move. The words stuck in her throat, and she suddenly felt each one of those six drinks pounding away in her brain. "I...I don't. It's just undignified, is all." A quiet sigh slumped her shoulders, and she bowed her head in defeat. "She doesn't even know him."

"Uh-huh." In a most uncharacteristic move, Tanya wrapped her arm around the princess' waist with an almost sisterly smile. "You know, you never got a chance to tell me what happened in the woods that night we were in Vale..."

An icy chill stole across Katerina's face as her mind drifted back to that beautiful and terrible evening. To the moment where it seemed like all the happiness in the world was right there at her fingertips. To the moment when everything went wrong, and it all shattered. "Nothing happened," she confessed quietly. "If anything had, I think... well, I think it's over."

Tanya's brow creased with concern, and the supportive arm tightened. "It didn't look like anything was over tonight," she ventured hesitantly. "It didn't look like anything was over when he grabbed you after the monks dragged us all inside. He wouldn't let you go. I don't think he *could*."

Katerina fell silent as she thought it over. She had played the moment back again many times herself. How the two of them had come together like magnets. How she felt his lips brush across her hair in a secret kiss. It felt the same as when they were back in the woods, when he'd tilted up her chin and kissed her under the stars.

...right before he walked away.

She opened her mouth to reply, unsure what exactly she was going to say. Then her head jerked up suddenly and she turned to Tanya. "Wait! How did you even see that? I thought you'd blacked out."

More than that, she *knew* Tanya had blacked out. She had a distinct memory of the girl's lifeless body being carried into the monastery. Cradled safely in Cassiel's arms.

For a second, Tanya froze as guiltily as Katerina. Then she blushed with a sudden grin. "How else was I supposed to get Cass to hold me?"

There was a moment of silence, then Katerina smacked her arm with a laughing shriek. "You *didn't*!"

"I most certainly did."

"You little sneaky bugger!" the princess cried, still laughing. "We were worried sick!"

"Hey, it was either going to be him or a monk." Tanya dodged the pillow flung her way with a mischievous grin. "There was no way I was able to walk by myself. I just... decided to go with the better-looking option. Coincidentally, the option that *didn't* take a vow of celibacy."

It was the proverbial straw.

Whatever tension had been left over from the bar, whatever lingering trauma, vanished clean away as the two of them dissolved into a fit of giggles. Loud, uncontrollable giggles. That kind that, once they started, they were unable to stop. It was as if that rational tether keeping them grounded had finally snapped, leaving them breathless and hysterical in its wake. Rocking back and forth as they clung to each other, the flood of alcohol in their system washing away the stress.

There was no end in sight. They were still going strong several minutes later, when there was a quiet knock on the door. A second later, it cracked open to reveal a familiar face.

"Guys..." Dylan began hesitantly, watching their every move, "is everything okay?"

For whatever reason, that just made them laugh harder.

They shook their heads and covered their faces as he slipped inside and bolted the door behind him, torn between a diagnosis of alcohol-poisoning or mere insanity.

"I was just..." He shifted uneasily, looking as though he'd rather go back outside and face down the royal army than deal with whatever mystical girl nonsense this was. "I was just making sure that everything was all right..."

The laughing only got louder, and he took a hasty step backwards.

"I'll actually just go—"

"No," Tanya resurfaced with a gasp, "you stay. I'm going to go." She pushed off the bed and hobbled towards the door, flashing the princess a mischievous wink on the way out. "See what kind of 'holy vows' I can break tonight. Wish me luck, Kat."

Dylan turned and stared after her curiously while Katerina made a hasty effort to pull herself together, smoothing her dress and drawing in deep breaths as the color began to fade from her cheeks. She was almost completely under control by the time he turned back around.

"Holy vows?" he asked her.

An echo of laughter danced through the princess' eyes as she thought of Cassiel, sleeping obliviously just a few doors down. Completely unaware of the heap of mischief headed his way.

"You don't want to know."

"Yeah," Dylan chuckled nervously, "you're probably right."

They stood there awkwardly for a minute. Her, staring down at the bed. Him, running his fingers back through his hair. Then he flashed a tight smile and reached for the door.

"Well, I guess I'll just—"

"Yeah, you should go."

Even though it had been his idea he froze in place, retracting his hand the instant she seconded the notion. His eyes made a brief scan of her face before a flush of color flooded his cheeks, leaving him as close to blushing as the princess had ever seen. "Kat, about tonight...I don't want you to think—"

"What?" she interrupted, staring evenly into his eyes. "You don't want me to think what?"

Again, the sudden spotlight threw him, and he paused uncertainly, looking as though he wished he hadn't decided to check up on the girls after all. He shifted uneasily from side to side, dark hair spilling into his face, and when he could put it off no longer he finally lifted his eyes. "I didn't want you to think that I'm interested in that girl," he said quietly.

This time, it was Katerina's turn to be thrown. She had expected a bit of a back and forth. A passive- aggressive dance that would leave them both exasperated and alone. If there was one thing she hadn't counted on—especially from Dylan Aires—it was the truth.

Typical that he chooses tonight...

She was worried the alcohol would work against her. Freeze her tongue or make her fumble when she needed to be strong. But it turned out to be quite the opposite. A wave of confidence flooded through her as she pushed to her feet, lifting her chin to look him right in the eye. "And why would I care if you were interested in some girl?"

It wasn't a question so much as a challenge. Throwing the ball back into his court. Forcing him to confront all those things he'd failed to say that night in Vale. Forcing a resolution.

Whatever that might be.

Dylan bowed his head for the briefest moment as some indecipherable emotion clouded across his face. When he looked back up a second later, he was subdued but calm. "I'm glad you're all right."

Katerina blinked in surprise as he turned back to the door.

That's it? He's just going to leave?

"You are bloody unbelievable!"

She hadn't meant to say it out loud. Or maybe she had. The whiskey was making it hard to be sure. Either way, he pulled back like he'd been burned, turning slowly around to face her.

"Excuse me—"

"Why didn't you tell me that you'd been here before?"

It fired out before she could stop it, surprising them both. She'd meant to ask about the shifter. Or Vale. Or the hunting expedition. Or any number of other seemingly important things. Instead, her drunken mind had settled upon this. And latched on with a vengeance.

"What's the matter, Aires? Can't decide which story to tell?" Her eyes gleamed with months of pent-up frustration as she repeated the question. "Why didn't you say you'd been here before?"

This time, his shock was undeniable. That impenetrable calm had shattered, and it was written all over his face. For a moment he simply stood there, trying to come up with something to say. Then, without seeming to think about it, he took a small step back. "I...I haven't."

"Don't lie to me," she snapped. "Dylan, it couldn't be more obvious."

They'd never gone head to head before.

Never had she stepped up and refused to back down. But the tables had turned. She wasn't a lost little girl running around in the woods anymore, waiting for him to save her. Things had changed. *She* had changed.

"I don't know what you want me to say." He lifted his hands in the air and spoke with such sincerity that, if she hadn't known better, she would have sworn he was telling the truth. But, even as he did so, he took another subconscious step back. "Kat, I've never been to this monastery."

It was an incredible thing. The way he could look her right in the eyes...and lie.

She took a step forward, making up the distance they'd lost. Bringing them close enough that she was standing just a few inches away. Close enough that she could slap him. Or kiss him. At this point, she wasn't sure which she wanted more. Then her shoulders dropped with a little sigh. "I thought you respected me more than that."

She might as well have slapped him. His eyes tightened with visible pain as the walls seemed to close in around him, leaving him breathless and unsure. For a split second he reached out as though to take her hand, then he remembered himself and dropped his arm back to his side.

"Kat, I can't..."

He trailed off, looking utterly lost as he stared down at her face. There was a battle raging behind those beautiful eyes, one she couldn't hope to understand. But, apparently, it was one that tipped in her favor. A second later, he crossed behind her and sat down on the edge of the bed.

He bowed his head with a quiet sigh. It was time to come clean.

"It was years ago when I came here. I was very young."

He spoke softly, keeping his eyes fixed on the floor. When Katerina sat beside him on the bed, it barely registered. He was lost in the past. His troubled eyes seeing things she couldn't.

"I was lost, alone. Had no practical skills of any kind. No way to take care of myself." A tiny shiver ran down his arms, but he didn't notice. "Completely at the mercy of the world around me."

It wasn't until Katerina's lips started to tingle that she realized she was holding her breath. It was almost impossible to imagine. This younger, vulnerable version of Dylan. In her mind, he had been a knife-swinging toddler. Sure of himself from the minute he took those first steps.

But the story wasn't finished yet. In fact, it was just getting started.

"Michael took me in. Raised me as well as he could. Gave me an education. A family." His voice tightened involuntarily at the last word. "A home."

The princess was spellbound. Utterly entranced. In truth, she had never actually expected him to cave. The Dylan she knew never gave even a bit more of himself than was required. Never revealed any more than he wished. And *this*? To finally come clean...only to reveal *this*?

"I don't understand," she interrupted quietly. "I thought you said your mother was the one who taught you—"

"She did," he replied quickly before just as quickly shutting down. "She did an incredible job...for as long as she could."

Another huge gap. Another giant hole where a chapter of the story should have been. But Katerina didn't press. Not about that. She had some experience with absentee mothers herself.

"It must've been a huge relief," she prompted gently. When he shot her a blank look, she was quick to explain. "After being out on your own for so long...to come here and find people to look after you. To find yourself somewhere safe."

He laughed shortly, but it never reached his eyes. "Not really. I hated it here." He laced his fingers in front of him, elbows resting lightly on his knees. "It was safe, comparatively speaking. But it was a cage. A beautiful, suffocating cage."

"So why did you come?" Katerina asked curiously. "Or, I guess more importantly, why didn't you just leave? It's not like the monks were keeping you here."

A muscle twitched in the back of his jaw, and she suddenly wondered if that was true.

"There was no leaving," he said shortly. "Back then, there wasn't a bridge yet to the outside world and I couldn't shift well enough to make it down the mountain on my own. I was stuck."

An interesting point, but it begged the obvious question...

"If there wasn't a bridge, how did you get here in the first place?"

For a second, he looked completely undone. Like that lost little boy had suddenly come back. Then he lowered his eyes back to the floor. "By a way that's no longer open to us."

His tone effectively ended the line of questioning, but for the first time Katerina felt as though that was one answer she might already have. She remembered the note the fairies had told her to deliver. The one Dylan had thrown away and had no idea the princess had read.

I remember a little boy who once needed some help himself...

Is that what the fairies were talking about? Had they taken a young Dylan to the sanctuary?

"At any rate, the second I knew I couldn't leave that's all I wanted to do."

Katerina could understand that feeling very well. And, given the nomadic restlessness that ran through Dylan's veins, she could only imagine how it must have been for him. Given the restless way his foot was bouncing up and down, she could only imagine how it must be for him now.

"Well, that's perfectly normal," she said sympathetically. "The claustrophobia. The feeling of being trapped. I feel that way right now—"

"No, it was more than that." His soft voice brushed lightly over the stones, painting a picture and taking the princess along with it. "I wasn't...I wasn't in a good place the first time I came here. And it wasn't just the monastery, it was a lot of things. I was only fourteen. My entire life had fallen apart, and I..."

He bowed his head suddenly, spilling his dark hair into his eyes.

"Michael tried to help me. He was patient and kind. He was better than anything I could have deserved." A wave of fondness automatically lit his eyes before darkening away. "But I didn't want help. I just wanted to leave. More than anything...I just wanted it to end."

It was quiet when he finished speaking. It was quiet for a long time. Then, when it became clear that the he was in a world all to himself, Katerina reached over and took his hand.

"So, what happened?" she asked in a whisper. Almost too afraid to say the words out loud. It wasn't the kind of story to have a happy ending. "How did you get off the mountain?"

"Easy."

He glanced down at their hands for a moment before pushing to his feet.

"I jumped."

Chapter 5

There aren't too many places a conversation can go, after one of the participants freely admits to having jumped off a cliff. Dylan left soon after. Leaving Katerina to lie awake in her bed for hours, staring at the ceiling, trying to process everything he'd said.

He'd left without saying a lot. Like how he'd survived, for instance.

She'd seen the drop from the monastery cliff a lot closer than she would have cared to, and she knew first-hand that one did not simply walk away if one were to fall. It was thousands of feet up in the air, with nothing but a carpet of jagged limestone boulders to soften your landing. To jump would mean an automatic death sentence, and yet Dylan had survived to tell the tale.

He'd also left without explaining what he meant about the shifter.

Katerina had put all her cards on the table that night in the woods. She'd told him she was falling in love with him around the same time that he was reaching up her skirt. It was literally the most vulnerable and intimate thing she could have done...and he'd walked away.

Much as she hated to admit it, the message was clear enough. He simply didn't feel the same way. And yet, every day he was doing things that seemed to prove otherwise. Whether it be those secret shared moments when they were curled up in bed, the fact that he couldn't seem to stop kissing her wherever they went, or the moment in the courtyard where he'd basically come back from the dead just to gather her up in his arms.

Then there was last night. 'I didn't want you to think I was interested in that girl.'

What the heck was she supposed to make of that?! Furthermore, wasn't the girl in the relationship the one who was supposed to play games? She may have been mistaken, having never done it before, but she was fairly sure that, as the woman, it was her right to play with him for a while. To jerk his emotions back and forth with a kiss and a smile, while she decided if this was something that *she* really wanted to do.

Why was *he* the one playing games? What gave *him* that right?

A group of giggling children raced past on their way to morning mass, rousing the princess from her deep trance. She pulled her cloak tighter around her shoulders, casting them a quick smile as their little feet pattered over the uneven cobblestone. The echoes of the bell summoning them to the sanctuary were still lingering in the crisp morning air. Funny, she hadn't heard it ringing.

Unable to sleep, she'd ventured out of her room and up onto the stone parapet overlooking the cliff where she and her friends had gathered the previous morning. With nothing but starlight to illuminate the landscape, she'd been unable to see anything more than the night sky. But as the sun crept higher and higher, inching its way towards dawn, she was able to extend her gaze farther. Over the endless mountain peaks. Out across the breathtaking vista.

...across the ravine and to the army waiting on the other side.

"At this rate, we should start paying you."

She whirled around with another start, surprised and a little nervous to see Michael walking towards her across the stones. He moved with the easy grace of one no longer burdened by the toils of time. The prayers and classes of the monastery ran to the chime of the clock, but otherwise the sanctuary moved to its own schedule. Set above the rat race that consumed the rest of the world.

"I'm sorry?" she asked nervously, unable to shake the feeling no matter how graciously he smiled. The man was a force. She couldn't help but stand a little straighter.

He smiled again, the warm light of morning twinkling in his eyes.

"For security." He gestured to her perch on top of the wall. "I don't know if I've ever seen someone keep such a vigilant watch."

"Oh, right." A blush stole across her cheeks as she hastened to climb down. It was easier said than done. Shod only in thin leather boots, her feet had nearly frozen where they'd stood. It seemed time had gotten away from her after all. Maybe it was a monastery thing. "Not me, I'm afraid." She offered him a shy smile, tucking her hair behind her ears with trembling fingers. "Just along for the ride."

The monk tilted his head to the side with an endless sort of patience, a flicker of curiosity dancing in his eyes. "I highly doubt that. We all have our part to play. Our way to contribute."

I wish very much that that were true.

Another blush stole across the princess' cheeks, and she quickly change the subject. "I was just admiring the view. It's different here than what I'd imagined. Beautiful and very...quiet."

Despite the staggering view, it was the quiet that struck her most.

This was a girl who'd come from the hustle and bustle of the castle. Whose childhood home boasted no fewer than one hundred noisy people at any time. She shared her chambers with half a dozen other women. She feasted every night at dinner with musicians, and entertainers, and the rest of the court. Never had she known such silence. She'd never known such complete isolation.

But standing there now, gazing out over the exquisite mountain peaks with the wind in her hair and the sun on her face, she had to admit it wasn't entirely unpleasant.

Michael chuckled and came to stand beside her. "Yes, that doesn't surprise me. Most people who come here are struck by the quiet. It takes some getting used to. At some point or another, most of them find themselves up here."

Katerina nodded, but a sudden chill swept across her arms.

Was this the place Dylan had been standing when he jumped? Was it a morning just like this one when he decided to take his own life? Another chill rocked through her body as her eyes darted up to the roof, remembering the look on his face as he gazed out over the cliff. Remembering the easy and habitual way he'd settled himself down upon the tiles. A place he'd sat many times before. "Was Dylan struck by the quiet?"

Michael glanced down in surprise before that twinkle came back and he looked at her appraisingly. "Someone's been doing her homework."

She blushed again but said nothing. Waiting for the monk to answer or not, as he chose.

"Yes, Dylan was struck by the quiet." Michael gazed out over the vista with a far-off look in his eyes. "But it didn't bring him peace, the way it does to most. It brought him conflict instead."

"What do you mean?" the princess asked, staring up at him with wide eyes. "What conflict?"

Michael glanced down again, but this time his face warmed with a quiet chuckle. "That story isn't mine to tell. Nor is it yours to hear. Only in his own time."

She should have been embarrassed, but something in his face didn't allow for it. Instead, the two stood there in a comfortable silence, gazing out over the snowy peaks.

"In the meantime, no one stays at Talsing without giving something back." Her eyes shot up nervously to his face, but he shook his head with that same steady calm. "I don't mean money. I mean a skill, your time. Everyone has something to give, Katerina. Whether they know it or not." The wind picked up around them as he lay a gentle hand on her shoulder. "Don't underestimate yourself, young one. You have a lot to offer." His eyes twinkled as they gazed down into hers. "You just need to find out what that is."

A sudden feeling of warmth stirred deep inside her chest. Right beneath the smooth skin where her mother's pendant used to hang. She reached up to touch it automatically, unaware of the fact that Michael had been intently watching every move.

"Make use of your time here," he continued. "The resources of the monastery are at your disposal. May I suggest the library," he added suddenly, "as a good place to start?"

Their eyes met again as he looked down with that signature twinkling smile.

"In the meantime, there's no reason in the world you shouldn't be able to take care of yourself. No man or woman at Talsing is just *along for the ride...*"

As if on cue the doors opened, and a group of well-armed teenagers flooded out into the courtyard. They didn't notice their two-person audience and didn't waste a moment's time as they split off into pairs and began to spar.

Katerina's eyes widened as she watched them, trying to imagine herself among their ranks, when they parted suddenly as a handsome man swept through the middle. A man who'd spent the better part of his night drinking, then taking an unwanted journey down memory lane.

He needed only a moment to find her. His eyes seemed conditioned by now to pick out her flaming red hair. A second later, he was cutting rudely through the practice session and heading up the steps to meet her. It was only when he got closer that he noticed Michael standing by her side.

Well, this doesn't bode well.

It was like watching a man get hit with a sedative. Freezing in place. There was a profound hesitation in his step when he saw the two of them standing together, and for a second Katerina thought he was going to turn right back around.

Then, with a sudden look of determination, he swept up the stone steps.

"What's this?" he asked with no preamble. "Private meetings on the terrace?"

Katerina shot him a look, chiding him for his rudeness, but Michael only laughed.

"They're only 'private' to those who insist upon sleeping through the bell." His eyes twinkled merrily as they swept his young protégé up and down. "A habit I see you've yet to break."

Dylan's face flushed, but he stood his ground. Granted, he seemed physically incapable of meeting the man's eye. Neither could he meet Katerina's.

"Don't you have a prayer circle to run?" he muttered. "Alms to give to the poor?"

Michael laughed again but began to make his way down the terrace. "I see those elusive manners have yet to materialize as well. Have a good day, children—I'll see you at dinner." He reached the bottom of the steps and was about to vanish through one of the doors, when he turned back, staring right at Katerina. "Remember what I said. There is a reason that you came here, child. A reason you were given this time. Don't waste it."

Without another word, he disappeared. Leaving the two teenagers standing in silence.

For a moment, Katerina wasn't sure what to do. She and Dylan hadn't exactly left things on an easy note; between that and Michael, she didn't want to anger him now. But when she finally got up the courage to glance at his face, she was relieved to see he was smiling.

"Good morning."

Her entire face brightened in response, warmed by the mere sight of it. "Good morning yourself. I wasn't sure if..." She shook her head quickly, stopping herself before she could begin. "Good morning."

He laughed lightly, turning his back deliberately on the people practicing in the yard before making his way up the steps to join her on the parapet. Despite everything he'd confessed the previous night, he seemed completely at ease. And, despite the fact that the sight of him standing on a ledge was giving Katerina a mild heart attack, he glanced over the side, then turned back to her with a smile.

"Are you avoiding them, too?"

She blinked quickly, trying her very best to appear nonchalant. "Sorry?"

He studied her face for a moment, reading between the lines, before glancing back down with a grin. "I forget, not everyone is cursed with hearing like mine."

Her brow furrowed in confusion, but a second later she figured out what she meant. For the second time that morning the door swung open, and Tanya and Cassiel made their way out into the courtyard. One, looking quite pleased with herself. The other, looking quite pleased in general.

They glanced around for a moment before spotting their friends and hurrying up to meet them beside the wall. Tanya was carrying a piece of toast in both hands. Cassiel had the coffee.

"Good morning," he said with a sparkling smile, offering a mug to each of them. "And how did everyone sleep last night?"

Katerina bit down on her lip to keep from grinning, while Dylan shot him a strained look.

"More than you did, from the sounds of it."

The fae flashed him a completely unapologetic smile while Tanya linked her arm through Katerina's, settling down to eat breakfast on the stone bench. While neither girl made direct eye contact, there was a series of secret sideways grins as they each nibbled on a piece of toast.

That's one way to stake your claim.

Of course, the princess did it by forcing the object of her affection to bare his soul and relive the dark horrors of his past. But to each their own.

"So, what's on the agenda for today?" she asked, feeling significantly more cheerful than she had that morning. "Kite-flying? Making rude banners to wave at the army—"

"Actually," Dylan shot her an apologetic look over the rim of his cup, "Cass and I were going to meet up with some of the shifters and start organizing a group to head to the village."

Both Tanya and Katerina set down their toast at the same time. In the after-effects of the booze, they had quite forgotten that there was a plan brewing to keep the monastery up and running. And they had quite forgotten that they were not a part of that plan.

"Some of the shifters, you say?" Tanya asked sweetly. Cassiel was deliberately avoiding her gaze. "Well, that's funny, because it just so happens that I'm a shifter myself."

Katerina poked her in the ribs. *Traitor.*

Dylan's lips twitched up in a fond smile before he shook his head gently. "All the shifters that don't have a broken leg. You need to take it easy, Tan. Rest up. Get back your strength."

"Not to mention, you don't shift into an animal," Cassiel continued apologetically. Katerina was surprised he'd dared to speak at all. But their men weren't exactly the timid type. "I don't think there's a way to make it down that cliff in a human form."

Tanya's eyes cooled, and she looked like she was doing some serious re-planning of her evening agenda. "What does that say about you?"

There was a beat of silence.

Then Cassiel brightened with a coaxing smile. "That I'm a woodland prince capable of doing just about anything?"

Another beat of silence.

Then Tanya smiled in return. "A woodland prince capable of warming his own bed tonight?"

The fae's lips parted uncertainly, but Dylan swooped in for a save. "Actually, there's a project getting started I thought you two might be interested in. Rebuilding the bridge."

"The one that Katerina cut down," Cassiel added authoritatively.

The princess' head jerked up. "What? *Me*?"

"Yeah, we took a group vote and decided to blame that on you last night at the bar." Tanya took a sip of her scalding coffee. "Sorry."

Katerina rolled her eyes and folded her arms firmly across her chest. "Fine. Well, how exactly are we supposed to rebuild this bridge that *I*, so arrogantly, hacked into bits?"

Dylan's eyes sparkled with scarcely contained laughter.

"A group of monks is already gathering the supplies. Just rope and planks of wood. A lot of people from the village are volunteering to help. The carpenters will show you all what to do."

Easy enough for even a princess to figure it out.

That's what his sarcastic smile meant. Katerina returned it full-force with a glare.

"Yeah, I remember what the bridge was made of, thanks." One day, she'd learn how to knock that smile right off his pretty little face. "What I *meant* was how are we supposed to set it up once the army is gone? It's not like we can just carry it over to the other side."

As it turned out, she knew how to wipe the smile off his face after all.

None of the others noticed the minute hesitation. The slight tensing of his shoulders. The way his eyes flickered without permission to where Michael was gazing out across the courtyard. By the time they'd looked around, he had cleared his throat and was looking back with a steady smile.

"They have ways..."

It was a rather mysterious way to end what had been a rather straightforward conversation, but Cassiel and Tanya were too concerned with caffeinating themselves to mind. Only Katerina looked back down at her mug with a sigh.

She couldn't be angry with him. They'd made too much progress last night; he'd opened up so much that she couldn't complain. All she wanted to do was understand.

Why did everything have to be so hard with him? Why couldn't anything just be as straightforward as it seemed? Was there ever going to be a time when she looked at him and found answers, instead of an unending series of questions?

No, probably not.

If only she didn't care so much. If only she could brush things off like the others, or be casual, the way Cassiel and Tanya were. Then maybe she wouldn't be stuck feeling like this all the time. Then maybe she could finally get a little—

"That's some nerve you've got."

Katerina and the others looked up in surprise to see a tall man standing at the foot of the steps, glaring up at them with four or five other people at his side.

"Looking down at the bridge you destroyed? Or the army you brought to our gate?"

Okay, games aside, I'm definitely not claiming credit for the bridge thing.

Katerina watched warily as the others slowly pushed to their feet. Dylan, in particular, was looking the man up and down, a flicker of dark anticipation dancing in his eyes.

"Not only have we apologized, but we've already worked it out with Michael." The words took on a hard edge as they flew through the air. "So, I'm not sure what else there is to talk about."

The man spat on the ground as an angry murmur filtered through his friends. "You think you're so special, don't you?" His teeth clenched with rage, and without him seeming to realize it his beefy hands curled up into fists. "You come here, bring this trouble to our house, and just expect to get away with it? Well, let me tell you something—it doesn't work that way."

Cassiel shot out a cautioning hand but Dylan slipped past it, ghosting lightly down the steps until he and the angry horde were standing face to face.

"Please," he said softly, "enlighten me, then."

For a split second, nothing happened.

Katerina sucked in a breath, Tanya set down her coffee, and Cassiel's eyes closed for the briefest moment before opening once more. Dylan, however, was standing perfectly still.

Then all hell broke loose.

"You BASTARD!"

It was hard to see who threw the first punch. Hard to make out much of anything in the blur of movement that followed. All the princess could tell for sure was all six men leapt onto Dylan at the same time. Leapt onto him with such fury she didn't see how he could possibly survive.

"Dylan!" she cried, sprinting down the steps without a thought as to what she might do next. Tanya was right behind, racing fearlessly into the fray, broken leg and all. "Dylan!"

There was a flash of color as Cassiel leapt off the parapet, racing to his friend's side. He didn't bother with the steps. Unlike the men they were fighting, he wasn't armed. But it hardly seemed to matter. The fae moved with such speed and skill that nothing could touch him. Twisting and turning. Punching and kicking. Until at last he reached the center of the horde.

"Enough," he panted, grabbing Dylan by the shoulders as he tried to drag him away. "This is no way to repay Michael's kindness."

But Dylan was beyond reason. Nor did he need Cassiel's help. The other flailing men might have leapt in on the action, but they had little to do with the matter at hand. This fight was between Dylan and the man who'd challenged him. No one else mattered. No one else even registered.

"Get Kat out of here," he ordered, dodging a punch as easily as if it was happening in slow motion. "Take her back to the rooms."

Cassiel ignored him, turning around swiftly to fight off the men coming from behind. More and more were joining every minute. A literal army against two lone men.

And two lone women.

Katerina jumped off the steps without thinking, landing squarely on the back of the nearest man. He straightened up in surprise as she wound her arm around his neck—the same thing she'd seen Cassiel and Dylan do a thousand times. Granted, she didn't have their strength, not enough to choke him out, but she was able to incapacitate him enough to get him out of the fight.

"Tanya!" she cried. "Get the guy in the blue!"

Despite the multiple weapons their attackers had brought to the fight, most all of them were still choosing to fight with their bare hands. All except a tall man in a navy cloak, who'd just charged straight into the brawl. He whipped out a knife at the same moment that he lashed it across Dylan's cheek—making the latter cry out in pain as he brought a hand to his face, turning around in surprise.

His face grew pale and his mouth fell open in shock.

"What the ..."

"Tanya!" the princess cried again, still holding on precariously to the man thrashing beneath her. "Get him!"

It was only then she realized that Dylan wasn't looking at the man in blue. He couldn't care less about the gash bleeding freely down his face. His wide eyes were locked on Katerina, staring as though he literally couldn't believe what he saw.

"Kat—" he began, then he was hit over the back of the head. He turned around with a violent curse and with two blinding strikes, he'd rid himself of his attackers and spun back to the princess once more. "What the hell are you doing?! Get down—"

A sudden sound cut through the clamor. An animalistic growl that had no place among men.

For a split second, the entire brawl came to a sudden stop as those who were fighting spun around slowly to look at the giant wolf standing in their midst. He'd come out of nowhere, leaving nothing behind but a pile of clothes and a lethal-looking blade. Katerina's eyes locked on the dagger before slowly returning to the wolf.

He clearly thought his teeth would do more damage.

At some unseen signal, all the men they'd been fighting suddenly melted away. Making a clear path between Dylan and the shifter. At the same time they circled around behind him, fencing him in. Forcing him to choose whether he wanted to finish the fight as a wolf, or as a man.

"Dylan, don't," Cassiel's quiet voice echoed from somewhere behind her. "These people mean nothing. Just dispatch the beast and be done."

A furious growl rippled through the crowd as his words, but Dylan didn't seem to hear them. His eyes were locked on the wolf. Staring intently. His shoulders rising with shallow breaths.

For a moment, he was tempted. His fingers twitched and the air around him seemed to shimmer with anticipation. Every muscle was tensed and ready. His eyes flashed with deadly fire.

But then, a second before he could make the shift, a heavy hand clamped down on his arm.

"That's enough, Dylan."

Oh, crap.

It was Michael.

In all the commotion, no one had seen him approach. If they had, the fight would surely have never gotten off the ground. As it stood, the crowd of grown men, each with fresh stains of blood on their hands, had turned a sickly shade.

Katerina released the man she was holding and slipped to the ground in shock, hoping desperately that the ancient monk wouldn't turn her way. She didn't think this was what he'd meant when he told her to find productive ways to fill her time.

But Michael only had eyes for Dylan. While Dylan had frozen dead still.

"Get inside," he commanded softly. "My office. We're going to have a little talk."

What would happen next was anyone's guess. In all their time together, Katerina had never seen Dylan heed the authority of anyone. He was his own person. Answerable to no one. It would be a cold day in hell before he pledged that allegiance to someone else.

But Michael wasn't just 'someone else.' And he certainly wasn't that to Dylan.

Without a backwards glance, the ranger did as he was told. Leaving the fight behind. Leaving the man who had wronged him bleeding in his wake. He didn't stop moving until he reached the door on the far side of the courtyard. It was there he paused for a moment before slipping inside.

Michael stared after him, an indecipherable emotion clouding his eyes. When he turned back to the hushed crowd, that emotion lingered. Freezing everyone in place. "This is not what we do at Talsing Sanctuary. I expected more from every person here." His eyes swept over the crowd before he shook his head and walked away. "This is not what we do."

The group stayed perfectly frozen until he'd vanished through the same door, and then for a moment or two after. Then, without a single noise, they quickly dispersed. Vanishing upstairs and down hallways. Back to their rooms where they could lick their wounds in private. Hang their heads in shame. Think about what they'd done.

In the end only Tanya, Cassiel, and Katerina remained. They alone didn't have a place they were supposed to be, but at the same time none of them wanted to stay in the courtyard.

"Back to my room?" Tanya said tentatively, after a minute of silence.

Cassiel glanced down suddenly, as if he'd forgotten the others were there, before he nodded his agreement. "Yeah. Sounds good."

Together, the two of them started off across the courtyard. They were almost halfway to the door before Tanya turned around and called back to the princess.

"Kat, are you coming?"

Katerina nodded her head slowly, but kept her eyes locked on the smears of blood staining the ground. "Yeah, I'll meet you there in a minute."

The others paused a moment, then slipped quietly through the door, leaving the princess standing alone on the wet stones. Her eyes glassed over as she replayed every violent moment in her mind. Shaken by the skill. Stunned by how quickly it had happened.

A gust of wind swept her hair around her like a fiery cloud, but even as she stood there a plan was forming. One that was just beginning to reveal itself, piece by piece.

Bridge-building will have to wait. Right now, I need to learn how to fight.

Chapter 6

Aside from Michael's mortifying intervention, there turned out to be another downside to getting into a fight at the Talsing Sanctuary; you had to see the people you were fighting every time you decided to open your door.

Katerina and the others kept a deliberately low profile for the rest of the day after the early morning confrontation. Skipping lunch. Ignoring the bell that summoned everyone to afternoon prayers. They planned to skip dinner as well, so Tanya shifted into one of the cooks they'd met earlier, and snuck supplies from the kitchen so the three of them could eat dinner in her room.

The three of them. Dylan had yet to return from Michael's office. In fact, neither one of them had been seen since that morning. A fact that was causing the princess no small degree of concern. The sanctuary was already rife with speculation that Dylan had killed their leader in some epic showdown. Either that, or Michael had cast him off the cliff to join what was left of the bridge.

Whatever the story tensions were running high, and the three friends felt it was best if they kept off the radar for a while. Keeping to themselves until curfew before heading straight to bed.

But Katerina didn't go to her room when the bell sounded. She made a little detour first.

"Hey, you still awake?" she whispered, knocking quietly as her eyes darted up and down the torch-lit hall. "Can I come in?"

There was a faint rustle of sheets, followed by the sound of light footsteps heading to the door. A moment later, a familiar voice filtered through the wall.

"I was wondering if I was going to..."

Cassiel opened the door with a radiant smile. A smile that was quick to fade.

"...see you tonight."

While he clearly wasn't expecting her, it was clear that he'd been expecting someone. His shirt was gone, his hair was artfully disheveled, and the glow of a dozen tapers lit the cozy room.

Despite the circumstances that had brought her, Katerina couldn't help but smile.

"Why, Cass, you flatter me!"

She slipped past him into the room, batting her eyelashes all the while. Taking in the sensual splendor as he cast a nervous glance up the hall and quickly shut the door behind them.

"Kat, what are...what are you doing here?" He crossed his arms a bit self-consciously over his chest. Not that it helped. The man was a living sculpture. The very definition of sex on a stick. Chiseled muscles. Flawless physique. Despite his attempts to cover up the candlelight still flickered tantalizingly across his bare skin, casting him in an ethereal glow as Katerina spun around on her heel, grinning ear to ear.

"Unless, of course, you were talking about Tanya."

He shifted his weight, looking as close to shy as Katerina had ever seen. "Did you need something? Is everything okay?"

She did need something. It was the entire reason she'd come. But although a part of her was vaguely aware she was undermining her own cause, she couldn't pass up such an opportunity.

"Wanted to *see* her, did you?" Probably not the word he was intending to use. "You didn't get to *see* her enough during the day?"

The arms came down with a dry look. In no possible dimension was the man shy. "Tell me what you want, or I'll drop you out the window."

The fae's sense of humor was better than most, but there were limits. You never knew when you'd crossed that invisible line. Katerina vaguely sensed it might be behind her.

"I need your help," she said plainly, getting straight to the point.

His eyes flashed with sarcasm. "You're off to a great start."

"I'm serious." In an act of supplication she perched tentatively on the edge of the dresser, ignoring the four or five candles that were placed there to set the mood. "Ever since I left the castle, I haven't been able to take care of myself the way I should. Sure, I've picked up some tips in terms of surviving out in the woods, but every time there's a fight I'm completely helpless."

She paused a moment, giving him the chance to disagree. But she knew he wouldn't. Cassiel wasn't one to sugarcoat the truth any more than Dylan was himself.

Sure enough, he simply stared back at her in the flickering light. Waiting for the rest.

"It's happened several times now," she said quietly, replaying each terrifying instance in her mind, "and then again this morning. I wanted to help. Wanted to protect the people that I..." Her voice trailed off and her throat tightened at the words she couldn't say. *The people that I love*. No, she couldn't say those words. But semantics aside, the fact remained. "...but I couldn't."

Her head bowed to her chest with a defeated sigh, then she lifted her chin once more. As determined as she was resolute.

"What happened today...it can't happen again. I won't let it."

Which is where you come in.

Cassiel had stayed very quiet during her speech. Reading between the lines. His bright eyes picking up on things that other people couldn't. When she was finished, he sat down on the bed.

"Why are you just deciding this now?"

It was a fair question. One she'd already asked herself many times.

"Well, I would love to have learned earlier than this. But at the castle, there was never any need. My brother was taught, but I was a girl. A female. My lessons were spent on... more specific things. *Like the crown. Like what I was to be like as queen*. She shook her head. "And from the moment I left, we've spent the days running. Running, and hiding, and trying very hard to keep to ourselves. It didn't seem like the right time to ask for fighting lessons."

Fighting lessons.

Just saying the words out loud sent sudden shivers racing over Katerina's skin. A fevered flush that was equal parts excitement and fear.

Cassiel was impassive. "And why are you coming to me with something like this, instead of Dylan?"

Another fair question. This one was more difficult to answer. In the end, the princess went for a half-truth. Praying like mad it would do the trick. "You know he'd never approve of anything like this," she answered in what she hoped was a reasonable voice. "The man about had a coronary when I tried to take out that shifter today."

For the first time, the hint of a smile danced across Cassiel's face. "To be fair, even I couldn't tell if you were trying to restrain him or if you simply wanted a piggy-back ride."

"That's what I mean," the princess insisted fervently. "I don't know *anything*." Her voice fell several octaves as she stared entreatingly into his eyes. "You've got to help me, Cass. Please."

The man didn't do favors lightly. But, at the same time, the two had struck up an inexplicable bond. He considered a moment, then lifted his head with a simple reply. "All right, then, I'll help you."

A surge of overwhelming relief almost lifted the princess off the floor. Just knowing that the fae was in her corner improved her odds by about a thousand percent.

"Perfect!" she exclaimed, leaping to her feet. "Where do we start?"

His eyes widened in surprise, looking at her eager stance. "Now? You want to start right now?"

She hesitated a moment, remembering the late hour. "Unless you had other plans..."

His dark eyes flickered regrettably to the door before he pushed to his feet with a sigh. "No, it seems that I don't."

As he went around the room, clearing things away and regrouping the candles so the place was better lit for training than for sex, she bounced eagerly in the middle of the floor. Now that the moment was finally upon her, the adrenaline was flowing and there was no way she could possibly sit still. She was about to say as much, when he glanced over his shoulder with a final question.

"I'm assuming you don't want me to tell Dylan about this?"

That made her pause.

The bouncing stopped as the smile froze on her face. She'd been so focused on simply getting Cassiel to agree to the task that it was something she honestly hadn't considered. Of *course*, that would be a problem. The men were like brothers. Why hadn't she thought of it before? "Is that—" she looked at him nervously. "Is that going to be a deal-breaker?"

"Quite the contrary," he replied cheerfully, pushing the bed back against the wall. "I enjoy keeping things from Dylan. It's one of the cornerstones of our relationship."

Of your completely dysfunctional *relationship...*

Katerina kept that little observation to herself and straightened up eagerly as he came to stand beside her in the center of the room. His eyes swept briefly over her, and he adjusted her stance the way one might move a puppet. Spreading the legs, angling the shoulders, squaring the hips.

When he was satisfied, he stepped back with a little nod. "All right, so, the first thing you want to know is—"

With a burst of adrenaline, she launched a wild punch at his face. He caught it with a look of surprise. She blushed a million times over. And for an awkward moment, they just stood there.

"—how to make a fist."

That smile came back again as he lowered it between them, then opened his hand so they could look at her own. At first, he clearly thought she was just messing with him. Then he held it up by the wrist, shaking it incredulously.

"What the heck is this?"

Her cheeks flamed bright red as she struggled to meet his gaze. "It's a fist."

He blinked, looking slowly between her and her hand. "You tuck your thumb under?"

She blushed again, but stared up at him with wide, innocent eyes. "To protect it." Even now, the finger was itching to take cover. "Otherwise, it could get broken."

There was a beat of silence.

It looked like it was taking everything the fae had to keep himself together. It looked like it was taking everything the princess had not to go sprinting from the room in shame.

But after a few seconds, Cassiel released her with a little smile.

"It's exactly the opposite," he explained calmly. "If you hit something like that with any amount of force, you'll break your hand for sure."

She glanced down nervously, trying it out the other way. "But wouldn't it just—"

"Here." He held up his palm with a look of endless patience. "Try it your way. Hit me."

It felt strange to be invited, but she did as he asked. Nothing happened.

"Harder." His lips twitched up, hiding another smile. "Like you mean it."

Again, she tried. Again, nothing happened.

It wasn't until he took her hand in his own, striking it against his palm, that she knew what he meant. He was as efficient as he was strong. Using just enough force that she felt the tendons in her finger start to tighten and stretch. She pulled back with a flinch, but before the pain could really register he released her, taking a step back and holding up his hand once more.

"Do you see what I mean?" When she nodded, he gestured her forward. "Now hold your hand the right way, and let's try again."

FOR THE NEXT TWO HOURS, Cassiel took her through the basics. It was a longer lesson than she could have hoped, and she absorbed more information than she could have possibly imagined.

The fae was a hard teacher. Hard, but fair. He never did anything unless there was a point to it, but he didn't shy away from the tough lessons either. On more than one occasion Katerina found herself flying through the air, only to come down hard upon her back. Each time, he would wait patiently while she caught her breath, then motion for her to get to her feet and try again.

She wasn't harmed. But she wasn't coddled either. Cassiel's style seemed to rest somewhere in the middle. He wanted to give the princess the confidence to try but prepare her for what she was in for at the same time. On that note, he didn't quite pull his punches...

"Seven devils!" she cursed, picking herself once more off the cold stone tiles. "You know, you could give me a little warning. I think you broke my spine."

"You think the royal army is going to give you a little warning?" he asked evenly. But he helped her up with a fond smile, brushing a piece of cracked limestone from her hair. "And I didn't break anything. That's something I very much would *not* want Dylan finding out about."

Katerina laughed, taking a half-hearted swing at him as the two circled around to begin sparring once more. "What's the deal with that anyway?" She surprised herself by dodging a punch, then countered quickly with one of her own. "One minute, you guys are bro-ing out. And the next, you're trying to kill each other."

"It's the only way we know how to love," Cassiel replied, tapping her beneath the chin to remind her to lift her eyes. "Look at my face, not my hands."

"I'm serious," Katerina giggled, hurrying to do as he asked. "The first time we met back at the hotel, I thought you were going to murder him right then and there."

Cassiel nodded, as if there wasn't anything unusual about that at all.

"Well, he deserved it." In a blur of speed so fast her eyes could scarcely follow, he slipped a hand behind her waist and flipped her once more into the floor. "Still does."

All the air rushed out of her body as she looked up at him with a rueful grin.

"But why? What could he have possibly done that was so bad?"

The quick back and forth came to a sudden stop as the princess realized she'd touched on a subject more delicate than what she'd intended. The sparring hands came down, and Cassiel paused in a moment of profound hesitation before turning his face away.

"He slept with my sister."

The silence that followed this simple statement was deafening. Getting louder and louder the longer it was allowed to go on. Finally, when it had become unbearable, the princess pushed to her feet with a quiet, "Oh."

For some reason, she would have never imagined Cassiel to have siblings. He didn't seem the type. And looking at the man now, she didn't want to imagine what heights of beauty any sister of his could attain. Still, it was hard not to ask the question.

Especially when it might answer so many of her own.

"So, he and your sister..." she paused casually, trying to act as though she was merely making conversation, "are they, like, a thing?"

Much to her surprise, Cassiel threw back his head with a sparkling laugh. It erased the tension still lingering in the room, and her heart slowed back down to a normal level. "It was years ago. Feels like another lifetime. So, no." His lips curved up the way they did whenever anyone used a phrase created after the turn of the century. "They are not *a thing*."

She nodded innocently, absentmindedly tucking her thumbs under as she raised her fists once more. Trying her very best to ignore the pair of piercing eyes that had fixed upon her face.

"Would it be so bad if they were?" Cassiel asked just as casually. He was circling around her with a hidden smile—a cat playing with its prey. "It might actually improve his mood."

Katerina opened her mouth to respond, but at the same time she remembered that Dylan once cautioned her it was impossible to lie to a fae. They always knew the truth.

Instead, she came at him with a question of her own. "When did you meet my mother?"

The pacing stopped at once. So did the smile. For a long moment, the two of them simply stared at each other. Then Cassiel bowed his head with the quietest of sighs. "I met Adelaide as part of a diplomatic envoy, shortly after she and your father got betrothed." His eyes drifted to the window as he remembered, lost in times gone by. "His position was fairly brutish and predictable, but she was the only Damaris I'd ever met who had a genuine desire for peace." Those eyes softened with a smile. A smile he turned towards her daughter. "Then again, she wasn't really a Damaris, was she? She was a Gray."

Adelaide Gray. The name had vanished when she married into the castle. Katerina hadn't heard it spoken aloud for a very long time.

She smiled back, somehow feeling both sad and happy at the same time. "You liked her?"

Cassiel's eyes warmed and he nodded. "Very much." The two sat down on the side of the bed, losing interest in their training session at the same time. "You actually remind me a great deal of her. Same eyes. Same...spirit."

Same spirit?

Katerina looked up in surprise. Talk of her mother had always been scarce. After her death, the king had refused to allow her name to be spoken. It made gathering information about the woman who was supposed to have raised her a lifelong challenge.

But the same spirit? By all accounts, her mother had been a firecracker. One of the only people in the world capable of putting her father in his place. A royal upstart who pursued her own agenda with such fierce passion that even the royal council was kept on its toes.

Much as she wished it was true, Katerina didn't see much of herself in that.

"Eyes, maybe." She tucked back her crimson hair with a wistful smile. "But I'm afraid the similarities stop at that."

Cassiel tilted his head curiously to the side, looking her up and down. "The girl who escaped an assassination attempt and fled the castle? The girl who braved an avalanche and took shelter in a giant's cave? The same girl who, for the last two months, has survived Dylan's ghastly personality and Tanya's cooking?" His eyes twinkled, and he shook his head with a little smile. "I wouldn't underestimate her."

A feeling of great warmth radiated out from the princess' chest; she ducked her head quickly, so he wouldn't see her grin. The fae may come off as haughty and intimidating to those who didn't know him, but he had shining moments as well. She would always remember this one.

"Come to think of it," she began coyly, "I think I *did* remember hearing something about the same girl throwing herself fearlessly upon a shifter's back..."

Cassiel nodded seriously. "Granted, I think he believed you were giving him a massage—"

"Hey!"

She shoved him as hard as she could, toppling them both off the bed in one fell swoop. Her head fell back in laughter at the look on his face—furious to have found himself on the floor—and she entangled her legs with his, purposely tripping him when he tried to get to his feet.

"You know how little effort it would take for me to snap your neck?" he threatened, kicking out with little regard as to where he made contact. "I'd be doing the world a service."

"Aww, you don't mean that." Katerina leaned against the base of the bed, settling into their fledgling brother-sister dynamic with a wide grin. "You'd miss me."

"I'd miss nothing," he spat, making a spectacularly failed effort to smooth down his messy hair. "The only reason I haven't already turned you in is that your brother didn't promise a reward."

The two paused their angry back and forth long enough to share a fleeting grin.

It was strange, the way things worked themselves out. It struck the princess, while sitting there, that in a different world she and Cassiel might have been considered a perfect match. Both heirs to a large and powerful kingdom. A natural joining of two great houses to guarantee peace.

...and wouldn't that have been a disaster.

"What are you thinking?" he asked inquisitively, unable to interpret her expression.

She flashed another grin, stretching out her sore and battered arms. "I was thinking what a nightmare it would have been if you and I had ever been forced into an arranged marriage. A prince of the fae, a princess of men. You probably would have been considered my top candidate."

Cassiel shuddered dramatically but stopped trying to escape her flailing legs and settled beside her on the floor with a grin. "It wouldn't have been so bad. As long as you didn't mind me straying away from your chamber from time to time."

"Oh, only from *time to time*?" Katerina repeated sarcastically. "We'd have to renovate the castle to add on rooms for your mistresses by the end of the first month."

He threw back his head with a sparkling laugh, one that settled in his bright eyes. "But you'd like them all, I swear. It could be a built-in friend circle. And, of course, you'd be free to see other people as well," he added graciously.

"Oh, well, thank you for that," the princess laughed, hitting him with a pillow.

"Aw, come on, Kat," he teased, playing as though it was real. "You know I'd still love you."

"...in your own anti-monogamous kind of way."

"Yes," he agreed brightly, "like that."

The two dissolved into laughter once more, when there was a quiet knock from the other side of the room. The door opened without invitation and Tanya stepped inside, pulling up short as she gazed down at the two of them in surprise. "Oh, I'm sorry. I didn't think the pillow fight started until later." She raised her eyebrows with an amused smile as they pushed hastily to their feet. "I'm not interrupting something, am I?"

"Not in the *slightest*." Cassiel gave the princess a not-so-discreet shove towards the door as his face cleared with a beaming smile. "I was hoping you'd stop by..."

The two shared a disgusting look as Katerina rolled her eyes, grabbed up her cloak, and headed to the door. They barely noticed she was leaving. It wasn't until she paused in the doorway that she turned back and caught Cassiel's eye.

Thank you, she mouthed, trying to convey everything she felt in just two simple words.

His eyes softened as he gazed back over the top of Tanya's head. *You're welcome.*

The two shared a fleeting smile, then he cocked his head pointedly towards the hall.

Now leave.

She closed the door behind her with a grin, head still buzzing from everything she had learned. From stealth attacks, to spinning kicks. Forbidden liaisons, to the background scoop on her mother. She was so completely caught up in the night's events, she didn't look where she was going and ran straight into something hard.

"Dylan!" she cried in surprise, looking up as a pair of familiar hands caught her. "Sorry, I wasn't..." She trailed off, trying to catch her breath. "What are you doing here? It's after curfew."

"I could ask you the same thing." His bright eyes flickered to Cassiel's door before coming back to her, looking profoundly uncertain. "Were you just—"

"Cass, Tanya, and I were just hanging out," she said quickly, emphasizing the second name as she tried to dispel any doubts. But, by the looks of it, she'd only made things worse. Her flushed skin, messy hair, and disheveled clothes couldn't be helping matters much.

His eyebrows lifted ever so slightly, and that hesitation froze him in place. "The *three* of you?"

Their eyes met for a split second, then his implication suddenly clicked.

"What—no! Eww!" she cried, torn between utter amusement and an intense gag reflex. "We were just...we were just eating a late dinner."

That was true. The three of them had eaten dinner together.

...five hours earlier, mind you.

"We've been trying to keep a low profile since what happened this morning," she continued pointedly, trying to shift the attention away from herself. "Sticking together indoors."

A faint blush colored the tops of Dylan's cheeks but, to be honest, it looked as though he was all flushed. Whatever had happened with Michael had clearly taken a toll, and he was either unwilling or unable to discuss it even a second longer.

Instead, he nodded swiftly and headed to his room. "That makes sense."

He turned to pull open the door, but the princess caught him quickly by the sleeve. Staring up with wide eyes as he turned around to face her.

"Wait a second...are you okay?" He might not want to talk about it, but the guy had been missing all day. And he looked like he'd seen a ghost. "I was worried about you."

That instinctual defensiveness faded slowly from his eyes the longer the two of them stared at each other. After a few seconds, he lifted a finger and stroked it across her cheek.

"No need to worry. Everything's fine."

A trail of goosebumps followed his touch, and she dropped her eyes quickly to the floor.

If she hadn't known where things had stood before they got to the monastery, they were a complete mystery now. Every word, every touch, seemed to have a thousand different implications, and after their impromptu confessional the previous night Katerina was firmly convinced that she was never going to understand the world of men.

She was about to slip away off to bed, when the hand suddenly disappeared.

"Actually—it's not."

Her eyes lifted in surprise to see him staring down with a glare. A mask of anger that did little to hide the layer of protective concern buried underneath.

"I don't know what you were thinking this morning, but you can *never* rush into a fight like that again." His hands gripped firmly around the tops of her arms, unaware that they'd been throwing punches the better part of the night. "The entire point of everything we've done over the last two months has been to keep you safe. That's not something I'll be able to do if you go rushing into a brawl with every shifter you happen to meet. You need to be smart. You need to be safe."

Oh, Dylan, you would not *like how I spent my evening.*

"Promise me." He was staring intently into her eyes, forcing her to meet his gaze. "Promise me you won't do that again. I need your word."

A little chill ran through her, but she lifted her chin and looked him right in the eye. "Then you have it."

He stared a second more before releasing her, looking satisfied. Without another word, he flashed her a quick smile and headed off to bed. She was quick to follow, not wanting to be caught in the hall after curfew. But a thrill of adventure stole over her as she vanished into the dark and uncrossed her fingers.

Sorry, Dylan. That's one promise I won't be able to keep.

Chapter 7

"Get up, princess. I didn't volunteer to waste my time."

No matter how many times she heard it, Katerina would never get tired of that encouraging voice.

Yeah, whatever. She pulled herself to her feet with a glare, wishing desperately she could wipe that teasing, cocky smile right off Cassiel's face. Unfortunately, it was a task easier said than done.

"You know, you should consider a career as an inspirational speaker," she panted, trying hard not to sound as out of breath as she was. "Tour the countryside, lifting people's spirits."

"You know, I would," he replied conversationally, "if only I could get past that pesky army who wants to shoot you in the face."

She lifted her head in disbelief, only to see a mask of theatrical concern.

"Details." He shook his head sadly. "They'll get you every time."

Over the course of the last two weeks, the two of them had fallen into a rocky rhythm. One that was equal parts bitter mockery and affection. Cassiel played hard and fought even harder. But Katerina was learning to keep up. In a way, it was like trying to outmaneuver your older brother. If your older brother was a famed warrior who had been alive for the last hundred and twelve years.

"You'd love that, wouldn't you?" She spun around and kicked him right in the jaw. At least, she would have if he hadn't caught her ankle. "If some random archer shot me."

"Katerina," he chided sternly, "I thought we agreed that if anyone got to shoot you it was going to be me. What do you think has kept me going all this time?"

Another spinning kick, followed by another deflection. At least this time she made contact. "You know once I get my throne back, I'm ordering your immediate execution, right?"

He grinned and rubbed his wrist, red from where her boot had smashed through. "And here I thought we were trying *not* to be like daddy."

Touché.

If someone had told Katerina three months ago that she'd be taking jabs and punches from a prince of the Fae, she would have thought they'd lost their mind. If someone then told her she'd be returning them with jabs and punches of her own...

"Good!" Cassiel dropped the banter at once and switched into his 'trainer' voice, flipping back into the air to avoid the princess' sudden attack. "That's very good, Kat!"

The last fourteen days the gang had spent at the monastery had been a mixed bag. On the one hand, they were safe, well-fed, and sleeping on what technically passed as a mattress for the first time in what felt like years. On the other hand, the army wasn't going anywhere, and that bridge the four friends had been building was going to have nowhere to hang.

Bridge-building. What a perfect metaphor for my life.

The second she landed back on her feet, Katerina glanced down at her fingers—rubbed raw from twisting endless yard of rope. She and Tanya had ventured over together the morning after the notorious courtyard brawl. At first, they'd been terrified that the people already working there would simply bound them with the same rope they were using to secure the planks and throw them over the side of the sanctuary wall. But it didn't take long to find the kindness in the hearts and minds of the villagers, the inherent goodness that had united them all along.

In a strange way, the whole thing reminded Katerina of that night in Vale. The celebratory bonfire, complete with every creature—supernatural or not—gathered under the sun. Trolls were hauling up armfuls of cedar. Goblins and dwarves were carving out the holes. Little swarms of pixies tirelessly laced the endless twine together, while the shifters and men strung the boards on through.

It was a team effort. A team made stronger by its diversity. A team so fantastical and welcoming and warm, they made Katerina wonder what the five kingdoms had been like before.

...before my own family ripped it apart.

"Heads up."

The princess looked up just in time to see a streak of blond and silver flying her way. It was all she could do to raise her hands before his legs caught around her waist, flipping her over onto the ground. He, of course, landed lightly on his feet. Staring down with a touch of amusement.

"Daydreaming, are we?"

Katerina stuck out her hand with a grin, forcing him to pull her back up. Yeah, the guy played rough. Every muscle in her body rebelled, and the second she was vertical she doubled over at the waist, crossing her hands in a defeated 'time-out.'

"When am I going to learn how to do that?" she asked finally, still dazzled by the effortless grace with which he moved his body. Still flinching when that staggering power was directed at her.

He raked his fingers through his hair, securing it in a little knot behind his head. "When you can stay on your feet for longer than five minutes at a time."

She opened her mouth for a scathing retort, then surrendered with a shrug. "...fair point."

It had become harder and harder to keep their nightly training sessions a secret as the days stretched slowly into weeks. They had to be done after curfew so as not to raise suspicion, there wasn't much space in their personal chambers, and the boy who lived next door happened to be a wolf gifted with supernatural hearing.

On only their second night practicing, Dylan had heard the commotion and rushed into Katerina's room, Only to find her and Cassiel panting on opposite sides of the room. In a blind panic, she'd made up a pathetic excuse about having seen a bat, and the entire thing dissolved into such a ridiculous jumble of lies that she and the fae didn't practice again for another week.

But recently, they'd solved that little problem.

Apparently, they weren't the only people at the monastery undergoing combat training. The monks held regular classes—teaching common people to defend themselves, and those gifted with magic to harness their powers—and they had taken to sneaking into one of the abandoned classrooms after the bell rang for curfew every night.

It was perfectly suited for such exercise. Padded floors. Mirrored walls. Plenty of space to spread out. By the end of the first night, the pair had upped what they were able to do about tenfold.

Of course, that meant Katerina's tired body was suffering tenfold the consequences...

"Did you really just call for a *time out*?"

Katerina snorted under her breath. Cassiel might try hard to blend in with the times, but the things at which he chose to take offense hailed back to an older era.

"What—they didn't have those back in the Middle Ages?"

Before she could straighten up, he flew towards her once more. This time he spun around at the last moment and came up behind her back, holding both hands hostage with one of his own as the other stretched slowly but surely across her neck.

"Don't panic," he soothed, gently strangling her all the while. "Think about what to do."

She tried to heed his words, but it was the most difficult lesson yet. The second his fingers pressed down on her windpipe, her brain shut down in borderline hysteria. Her lungs heaved and strained as they tried to gulp in even a breath of air, but his hand wasn't letting her.

She couldn't answer. She simply shook her head, eyes watering involuntarily as she tapped quickly on the back of his hand. It was their signal that a limit had been reached. A signal to stop. A signal that he'd honored every time.

Until now.

He glanced down impassively at her frantic tapping but shook his head. She felt the steady rise and fall of his chest behind her, breathing so easily while she could not.

"Not this time, princess," he said gently. "This is the most common attack used to incapacitate a woman. A lesson it is imperative for you to learn."

Her heartbeat jumped and skittered beneath his hand, but he spoke in a quiet, almost hypnotic tone. Taking her there with him. Centering her chaotic thoughts.

"All my weight is on my back foot, shifting our balance to the left. That's the only angle from which I can hold you. Now, calm down and think. What are you going to do?"

Weight on the back foot...angled to the left...

She tried to make sense of it. Tried to remember her training. But it was like trying to remember a dream after you'd already woken up. The longer she stood there, the faster it slipped from her fingers, the weaker her body got as she desperately fought for air.

She tapped on his hand again. Faster, this time. More urgent.

"I know you're panicking." His face came down beside hers; she felt his breath on her cheek. "I know all you want to do is run; the world's starting to go black. But I am the one off-balance here. I am the one in a vulnerable position. That puts you in control."

His hand tightened and the room spun.

"Now, what are you going to do about it?"

It happened before she was aware of it herself. Before she'd made the conscious decision to move. One second, she was standing there. Choking and desperate for breath. The next, the hand imprisoning her was gone. There was a quiet gasp as Cassiel went flying through the air before landing in a heap on the floor. Crumpled at her feet.

Holy suffering mother of hotspurs...

The room went dead quiet as the princess lifted a hand to her mouth.

Did I just do that?

Up was down. In was out. Black was white.

At first, she thought that Cassiel would be angry. They had been fighting for two weeks now, and he had never found himself the one smashing into the floor. But when he peered up at her a moment later, a beaming smile was stretched across his face.

"Well, look who finally decided to get in the game..."

The princess let out a burst of breathless laughter, thrilled beyond words, staring at her own hands like she couldn't believe what they'd done.

At the same time, the door opened behind them and a familiar cinnamon mohawk slipped inside. Tanya took one look at the scene in front of her before letting out a low whistle and lifting her hands for a round of congratulatory applause. "Well done! It usually takes a while to get him onto his back." She shot her boyfriend a mischievous wink. "Likes to be in control, this one..."

Cassiel got to his feet with a roguish grin as Katerina settled herself in one of the desks for a well-deserved break. Her throat was still throbbing from being held with such unrelenting pressure for so long, but no matter how hard she tried she couldn't seem to stop smiling.

I did that. He was choking the life out of me, but I managed to throw him off. Me.

"I wasn't going easy on her either." For his part, Cassiel seemed just as thrilled as Katerina was. He was gingerly massaging his shoulder where it had smashed into the stone, but his eyes were dancing with unmistakable pride. "She did it all on her own. If she hadn't been able to, I'd decided to give up the ghost entirely and just let her die."

The princess laughed as Tanya smacked him in the chest and fished something silver out of her bag. She'd vanished a few minutes earlier, promising to return with snacks. And while it looked as though she'd eaten them on her way back, she had returned with a stolen flask of whiskey.

"Well, cheers to that!" She took a huge gulp before passing it o the fae. "I don't mind admitting that I'd be pretty lonely up here at this monastery if you were gone."

"Oh, thank you." Katerina joined them in the middle of the room with a rueful grin. "I'd hate for it to be a nuisance if I had died—"

A spray of whiskey spat in between them.

The girl looked up in alarm as Cassiel lowered the flask away from his face, looking as though he'd recently been poisoned.

"What...the bloody Mary is this?"

Tanya brightened up with an instant smile. "Oh, I made it myself! Grinelda in the kitchens got me some stuff to mix together. I call it *the lost cause*." She nodded brightly at the princess. "In honor of your training sessions."

The princess had been in the process of reaching for it, but she dropped her hand with a scowl. At any rate, she could smell it from where she stood. A strange mix of kerosene, welding oil, and Carpathian gin.

Cassiel cursed, wiping his mouth with the back of his hand. "It's the most disgusting thing you've ever made—and, Tan, that's saying something."

The shifter snatched it back, lifting it up for a tentative sniff. "It's not so bad." Cassiel raised his eyebrows, and she recanted. "All right, fine. It's terrible. I was just excited that it was something stronger than spiced apple cider." When the rim of the flask began to bubble and melt, she lowered it with a wistful sigh. "I should have known when Grinelda offered to help. We all know she isn't exactly Team Damaris..."

Over the course of the last few weeks, the people of Talsing Sanctuary had divided into two groups: The people who supported the princess and her cause, and the people who thought the whole royal family was better off dead. Only Cassiel remained stubbornly on the fence.

Katerina remembered the exact moment it had happened. The moment when her royal secret had gotten out. Strangely enough, it hadn't even been her fault. It had been something Dylan had done. She and the others had been sitting in the dining hall, at a table all to themselves. Little by little they'd begun to ingratiate themselves with the rest of the villagers, but that hadn't yet extended to socializing during meals. And it all came to a screaming halt that day at lunch.

Annalisa, a young girl who worked in the kitchens, had just been walking over with a fresh tray of biscuits when the toe of her boot had caught on the wooden bench. Dylan jumped up to catch her just as she went tumbling, but in the process he leaned too far forward, and the queen's royal pendant slipped out of his shirt.

A literal hush had swept over the entire room as a hundred pairs of eyes locked upon the magical stone. Dylan realized what had happened a split second later and stuffed it back into his shirt, but by then, it was too late. The pieces had clicked together, and the eyes of the sanctuary drifted slowly from Dylan to the frozen girl sitting in their midst. The one with the fire-red hair.

The next few days had been rough, but surprising as well. For every two people who despised her, Katerina was able to find at least one willing to give her a chance. It was a ratio she was determined to change. Little by little. Bit by bit.

She spent her days slaving away on the bridge project—helping repair the damage in any way she could—and her nights slaving away at her training. Preparing for all the damage yet to come.

"Watch your left."

She looked up just in time to see Cassiel flying at her once more. Her arms flew up defensively and she was able to deflect his first attack, only to have him come at her from the other side, smashing her into the floor ten times harder than the fae had. Apparently, pride could only stretch so far. The shoulder was hurting and the fae carried a bit of a grudge.

"What did I say in the beginning?" he asked impassively, ignoring the plume of dust that had sprung up in her wake. "Never let your guard down."

The princess let her head drop back to the floor with a groan, blinking slowly as a host of stars danced dizzily before her eyes. "Actually, you assured me that you weren't as vindictive as you might seem. I should have known it was a lie..."

The world slowly came back into focus as he offered a helping hand. At the same time, a not-so-helpful voice chirped cheerfully from the sidelines.

"You know, maybe you would fight better if you didn't spend so much time on your back."

A rush of pain shot down the princess' legs as she pushed to her feet, and she shot Tanya a withering glare. Her contributions were never quite as encouraging as the shifter might think.

When asked about what Katerina had been doing in his room that first night, the traitorous fae had apparently decided to tell the truth. Tanya had been delighted by the entire notion and had immediately appointed herself in charge of the princess' morale. Since then, she'd spent most every night 'supervising.' Perched in the center of his bed, her leg propped up on a sea of pillows, calling out instructions and critiques through mouthfuls of popcorn as the two slaved away on the floor.

Cassiel found this inexplicably charming. Katerina did not.

"It's a shame that one ended with a punch to the face." The shifter grimaced as the fight continued once more but offered the princess a thumbs-up. "I thought you almost had him."

The princess spat out a mouthful of blood, determined to murder them both.

"You thought she almost had me?" Cassiel echoed with a suggestive grin. "I think you know it takes a little more than that."

Tanya flashed him a witchy smile. "...there's a lot of ego to work through first."

"Would you like to try?" Katerina interjected pointedly, cutting short their teasing before it could get off the ground. "You think you can do better, be my guest. If not, shut the... just shut up!"

Tanya paused a moment, actually considering, then shook her head brightly. "Yeah, I don't see either one of those things happening."

The princess' hands itched longingly for a blade, but the fae was quick to intervene.

"Let it go," Cassiel advised gently, beckoning her forward with a twinkling smile. "Trust me, I understand the impulse. But let it go."

Katerina rolled her eyes, but joined him in the center of the floor, marveling once again at how the shifter and the fae ever became a couple. On the surface, you couldn't imagine a worse match. But just as it was sometimes better to let a wildfire run its course, the two completed each other in a strange way. The passion. The lust for adventure. The string of psychological neuroses that would have sent most anyone else running for the hills.

When the book closed on Cassiel and Tanya, they'd either end up killing each other or they'd outlast them all. Dylan and Katerina were already placing secret bets.

"The two-part combination," Cassiel instructed, lifting his hands. "Do you remember?"

The princess thought back, then shook her head slowly. She remembered the broken finger from the first time she'd tried, but the salient details escaped her.

"Left-hand jab. Throw the elbow. Let the momentum carry you into a kick."

...and try not to break your finger.

"That's right," Katerina nodded quickly. "I remember."

These things usually happened very slowly. Despite his penchant for theatrics, Cassiel was a patient teacher and would always make sure she'd grasped the concept before shifting things back up to a normal speed. But this time, the princess was still riding high on adrenaline.

She'd just thrown a woodland prince into the floor. Victory was all but assured.

With a speed and recklessness that took them both by surprise she hurled herself towards him, throwing out the first jab in the process. It grazed the side of his cheek as he shifted to avoid it, but by the time he did she was already whipping around her elbow as she spun into a high kick.

She'd never really understood before—the thrill of the fight. The rush of exhilaration that came when you threw caution to the wind and met your opponent head-on. She'd seen it in other people, of course. Seen flickers of it dancing in their eyes. But she'd never experienced it for herself.

Not until that very moment.

With a breathless cry she lifted into the air, her crimson hair whipping around in a fiery arc as her leg flew out with blinding speed. He caught it just an inch away from his face, but the princess didn't stop when she'd landed. Cassiel was skilled enough that she didn't need to worry about hurting him, and she had several other moves that she'd been aching to try...

"Good!" he shouted encouragingly. "That's good, Katerina! Keep going!"

Together, the two of them danced across the floor. A graceful blur of deadly force as she put everything she'd learned to the test. Laying it all on the line. Matching him blow for blow. Tasting her own blood, though she was too elated to care. Kicking and punching and laughing and twirling until she spun around to a sudden stop...

...right in front of Dylan Aires.

Oh, crap. Maybe I should've had that drink after all.

Chapter 8

It was like all the air had been sucked out of the room. Like a shower of ice-cold water had poured down from the ceiling. Katerina felt the adrenaline itself cool inside her veins as she stood there before him, trembling like a school child caught cheating on an exam.

"This..." He took a step inside, gazing around the room with unconcealed shock. "*This* is what you've been keeping from me?"

Her cheeks flushed bright red, but she was unable to reply. She'd been a fool to think they'd just keep getting away with it. You didn't pull things over on a ranger. Let alone *this* ranger. At the same time, she realized they'd let themselves get quite a bit louder than usual. A moment too late, obviously. Dylan must've heard the commotion all the way down in his room and came to investigate.

"You haven't been avoiding me...you've been *training*?"

The word rang out like an accusation between them. Hard and sharp. Everyone, even Cassiel, dropped their eyes to the floor as Dylan shut the door behind him with a deafening bang.

Get it together. He's not in charge of where you go, or what you do. And even if he was, you're not doing anything wrong. You're learning to protect yourself. He should be thrilled.

But even as she thought the words, somehow Katerina knew it wouldn't be that simple. "The thing is, I didn't think that you'd..." Her voice choked out with nerves, and she had to start again. "I knew you wouldn't—"

"Your hand."

She might as well not even have been talking. Dylan certainly wasn't listening. He was coming to his own conclusions. Making his own decisions about what to do next.

"You said it had gotten caught in the rope. Working on the bridge..." His bright eyes flickered down to her recently broken finger, and she fought the urge to hide it in the folds of her dress. The first casualty of that two-part combination Cassiel had been showing her. The one she'd been so thrilled to have mastered, just a few short moments ago.

"Yeah." She tucked her hair behind her ears, stalling for time. "Dylan I just—"

But Dylan had heard quite enough. And he'd seen even more. Without another word, he walked swiftly to the center of the room and punched Cassiel right in the face.

"Dylan!"

There was a sickening crunch and Katerina's hands flew to her mouth.

She happened to know how hard it was to do exactly that. And she happened to know the precise amount of force it would take to make that unforgettable sound.

"Dylan, he didn't do anything! He was *helping* me!"

The fae hadn't made a sound, hadn't said a word. He'd absorbed the punch silently and was staring back at his friend with an unshakable mask of calm.

Dylan, on the other hand, was a bit more volatile.

"What the... what did you think you were doing?" His voice dropped to an angry growl as the two of them stood toe to toe. "Teaching her to fight? Throwing *punches* at her face?!"

Cassiel lifted his head calmly, ignoring the drip of blood trickling down his face. "You don't think she should know how to fight? How to defend herself? With half the world out to kill her?"

Dylan ignored the obvious logic of this statement, a willing prisoner of his own rage. "I *think* that with half the world out to kill her, she shouldn't be fighting *us*." It was like the princess wasn't even there. She might have been the one who'd begged for lessons—and she suspected Dylan knew this—but every bit of his anger was directed at the fae. "I *think* that, of all the people in the world, she should be able to count on *us* to protect her. To keep her safe from freakin' harm!"

With his every breath, he was itching for a fight. But Cassiel was far too practiced to get drawn into something like that. And he'd known his friend for a very long time.

"You're smarter than how you're acting. You're reacting right now," the fae replied quietly, both refusing to escalate and refusing to back down. "If we were talking about anyone else—"

"What the heck is that supposed to mean?!"

Yeah. What the heck is that supposed to mean?

"Guys?"

Tanya stepped tentatively between them, holding up a hand on either side. The men refused to budge, but Katerina shook her head discreetly from the sidelines.

Not now, Tanya.

To be honest, she didn't know if Dylan's patience could handle any more of the shifter's 'helpful' ideas. At this point, she wasn't sure if she could either.

"It means you're letting your feelings for this girl blind you to the obvious truth." Cassiel's eyes flashed, but he kept himself carefully under control. "She's in trouble. As much trouble as one person can be in on their own. She doesn't need three protectors—she needs a literal army to come stand at every side. *Every* little thing can help. *Every* little skill. And if you can't see that, then—"

"This coming from the guy who wanted to kill her just a few weeks ago," Dylan shot back angrily. "This coming from the guy who would've just walked away. The *only* reason you're still here is that you don't want to see her bloody brother on the throne!"

Katerina flinched, feeling each word like a physical blow. Was that true? She'd never understood why the three of them had been so quick to pledge their loyalty—the fae especially. At the time, they'd been living every moment under constant threat, so she'd been too grateful to ask.

Was that all there was behind it? That she was the lesser of two evils compared to Kailas?

Cassiel took a deep breath and dropped his eyes to the floor. Gathering his thoughts. Trying to sort through a century's worth of conflict in just a few seconds time. For a moment, their little world seemed to stand still. Then he took another breath and lifted his eyes. "That's how it started, yes. For both Tanya and for me."

Without seeming to think about it, he reached out his hand. The shifter slipped hers inside without a second's pause. The two of them stared solemnly back at Dylan.

"I would've done anything in my power to keep Kailas from ascending to the throne. I would have given my life to stop it. Helping his less dangerous twin sister seemed a small price to pay."

Less dangerous twin sister. So, I'm simply the better alternative. Thanks, Cass. Thanks a bunch.

"But then we got to know Katerina," Tanya said suddenly. Despite her precarious position, poised in the middle of a fight, she stood there without a hint of fear. "Every day, every night. We spent the next three weeks wondering how a girl like her could possibly have Damaris blood."

"A girl delighted by the supernatural," Cassiel continued quietly. "A girl who would follow a crying child into the woods. She gave me her cloak that day after the storm..." His eyes softened, and his voice trailed off as he remembered. It was one thing to feel something in the moment. It was another entirely to put it to words. When he looked back up a moment later, that age-old conflict was finally settled. Damaris or not, he was suddenly sure. "I might have stayed because of Kailas. But I didn't walk away because of Katerina."

Aww, I love you, too, Cass. Like a brother. Well, not like my brother. He's evil.

More than anything the two had shared in the practice room those last few weeks, more than anything that has passed between them, it was those words that touched Katerina the most. Her eyes watered but she lifted her head high, more determined than ever to deserve his allegiance.

But the fae wasn't finished yet. He had one final blow to deliver.

"But that's not the real question, here, is it?"

The ranger lifted his head, looking as though he'd been shaken from a trance. Whatever he'd expected to find going on in this room, the trio was confounding his every expectation. After an open pledge of support to Katerina, he apparently didn't know what could possibly come next.

Cassiel's eyes danced as he turned from the ranger to the princess.

"Why did *you* stay, Dylan? Why didn't *you* walk away?"

IT WAS A GOOD THING the supply run the shifters were planning was happening in the next couple of days. At the rate the men were drinking, the entire monastery would soon be bone-dry.

"Do you think maybe you should slow down a little?" Tanya asked casually, looping a finger around the bottle to pull it discreetly out of reach. "Save some for the rest of the planet?"

Two pairs of hands shot out to stop her, putting the whiskey back in the center of the table.

"No."

It was the first thing the men had agreed on all night.

After Cassiel's rather pointed question, the practice room had devolved into a kind of metaphorical cauldron. Simmering at a dangerous rate. Threatening at any moment to boil over. If the entire thing had taken that opportunity to spontaneously combust, Katerina wouldn't have been surprised.

Tanya had intervened with a universal solution. *"Let's get a drink."*

Of course, that had been about two hours ago. By now the entire table was littered with empty bottles of liquor and, judging by the men's unrelenting pace, there was no end in sight.

"Are you ever going to talk to me?" the princess asked quietly, angling herself so that only Dylan could hear. "Or are you just going to sit there and try to drink yourself to death?"

Maintaining direct eye contact, the ranger defiantly drained the rest of his glass—looking as though the second option was perfectly fine with him. Kat sat back in her chair with a sigh, but no sooner had she done so than he answered in a soft voice.

"You promised me."

There it was. The three words she'd been dreading since going to Cassiel that first night.

She'd expected it to be louder. Angrier. An accusation hurled with bitter venom across the table. But it wasn't. It was quiet. Almost too quiet to hear. A low murmur, with room for no other emotion than a heartbreaking kind of betrayal.

But that betrayal, however well-intentioned, was misplaced.

"I promised to be smart," she replied slowly. "I promised to be safe." *And I crossed my fingers.*

His eyes flashed up as his hand tightened around his glass. She didn't know how he could possibly be so steady after drinking so much. She didn't know how he could even be sitting up straight. But the man was a statue. Piercing right through her with those impossibly sky-blue eyes.

"You *promised* not to be rushing into any more fights. You *promised* not to put me—"

"I can't always count on you to save me!"

The others looked discreetly away as the rest of the bar suddenly went quiet. There weren't many people out at such a late hour, but those who were slipped quickly out of their chairs, heading discreetly to the door. The people of Talsing might have developed a natural Damaris fascination, but that didn't mean they wanted to be collateral in whatever explosion was on its way.

Dylan stared at her until the last customer had vanished, a thousand different emotions dancing behind his eyes. When he finally did speak, it was like he was dragging the words out of himself. From somewhere deep in the darkness, where even he didn't dare to go.

"You think you can't count on me to—"

"No, it's not that." She shook her head quickly, horrified by his misconception, desperate for him to understand. "You saving me isn't enough. I need to be able to save myself."

The ranger shook his head sharply, but before he could reply the others slowly pushed to their feet, returning what was left of the whiskey to the bar.

"Don't start, Dylan. You know she's right." Cassiel's tone was strangely sympathetic, but it warned his friend to back the hell off at the same time. "What's the alternative? That she does nothing to defend herself and waits every time to be rescued? If you really cared about her safety, you should have been the one to initiate this. Not her."

The argument opened right back up, but this time Cassiel was having none of it. He simply nodded goodnight to Katerina, then leaned down gracefully and punched Dylan in the face.

"That's for hitting me."

He and Tanya left without another word. Leaving the tavern completely deserted except for the princess and the ranger. Both of whom were glaring each other down.

The princess and the ranger...*and* an unlucky bartender. A man who looked like he'd been on the verge of having a full-blown panic attack since the four friends stepped inside.

The unlikely pair might have finally had some semblance of the privacy they so desperately needed, but that didn't make it any easier to say the words. For what felt like ages, the two just sat there. The clock ticked loudly between them. The tension was so thick it was hard to breathe. It had just reached a breaking point, when a trembling voice piped up tentatively from the corner.

"...you guys want some peanuts?"

Katerina and Dylan looked over at the same time, and the bartender nodded swiftly. Setting down his towel, he headed for the door.

"Yeah, I'm just going to go...be somewhere else right now."

The door clicked shut behind him and Katerina let out a quiet sigh. She didn't want to fight with Dylan. That was the last thing in the world she wanted. She only ever wanted to understand. But, as usual, they had found themselves right back in the middle of what felt like a perpetual war.

"Why are you so angry about this?" she finally asked, breaking the unending silence. "What could possibly make you so angry about me preparing myself for an eventual fight?"

He didn't miss a beat. And the answer sounded strangely rehearsed. "Because I can protect you."

Her temper frayed, and she slammed her glass down so hard that a little piece chipped off. "Cassiel's right—that's bull! This *only* helps, Dylan! It *only* helps to keep me safe!" All those pent-up emotions were coming to a boil. At any moment, they might burst free. "This fight is coming, and when it does I have to be ready! I have to be ready for whatever's going to—"

"BUT YOU SHOULDN'T HAVE TO!"

The room went dead quiet as she stared at him in shock. Panting as though he'd sprinted a marathon. That signature calm abandoned him as those wide eyes fixed desperately onto hers.

"This fight might be coming, but *you* shouldn't have to fight it!" he yelled. "You're innocent in all this, you've done nothing wrong! And to take that away from you—"

He cut off quickly, stopping himself before he could say anymore. Never had the princess seen him at such a loss for words. At such a loss of control. It was as if all those delicate little threads holding him together had finally snapped. Revealing the man that lay inside.

"You don't know what it's like." As loud as he'd been yelling, his voice was suddenly a hoarse whisper, barely making it across the table. "You don't know what it does to you. Family fighting family. The kind of scars that will leave. You'll *never* be rid of them. You can *never* get clean."

Katerina had no idea what to say. She was scared to even move. The brave hero who'd been holding her up since she left the castle didn't seem to realize that his hands were trembling.

"It's all happening just the way it did before," he murmured, running his fingers manically back through his hair. "We show up at the monastery for safe-keeping, now you're starting to train..." A violent shudder ripped through his whole body, and he tried to steady himself with a deep breath. "This *shouldn't* be your fight. And it doesn't have to be. There are things I can do to stop it. Things I can do to protect you from..."

The entire world seemed to freeze as their eyes met across the table.

"...from turning out like me."

Chapter 9

Katerina left Dylan that night in the bar. All their cards were on the table and there was simply nothing more to say. At the time, she didn't even know if he realized she was gone. He just stared at the little candle in the center of the table. His eyes flickering with the light of the flame. He wasn't going to talk any more. The vault had closed, and he refused to let her in. He seemed lost in the past—or maybe drowning in it. Whatever it was, she was done. If he wanted to live his life in riddles and half mysteries, she wasn't going to fight it. He would have to come to her.

The next morning, she got dressed quickly and headed straight out to the terrace to begin work on the bridge—deliberately skipping the four friends' morning meal. She was in no mood for hangovers and chitchat today. Nor did she want to overanalyze every word or gesture that Dylan threw her way. She already had quite enough to think about all on her own.

"It's all happening just the way it did before. We show up at the monastery for safe-keeping, now you're starting to train..."

She folded her legs beneath her and took a seat on the damp stone. No one else was out so early—they were still eating breakfast in the dining hall—but there was always plenty to do. With the practiced hands of one who'd done it many times before, she picked up a coil of rope and began weaving it methodically through the wood. In one hole and out the other. Again, and again.

You don't know what it does to you. Family fighting family. The kind of scars that will leave.

The wind picked up and blew a few stray tendrils of hair around her face. The rest was falling down her back in two thick braids. Pulled out of the way so she could focus on her work.

You'll never be rid of them. You can never get clean.

Little beads of sweat trickled down her cheeks as the sun climbed over the alpine peaks and beat down upon her shoulders. The rope was nothing more than a blur now. In one hole and out the other. Faster and faster. Again, and again, and again—

"You know it got your dress, right?"

The princess looked up with a start as a tall shadow spilled over the stones. She started with the shoes and squinted the higher up she got, until at last she got to a beautiful face. A beautiful face that was grinning down at her with two brightly-colored eyes. One brown, and one blue.

"My dress?"

Rose cocked her head and the princess looked down in dismay to realize the shifter was right. In her tunnel-vision haste, she'd threaded the rope right through a hole in the bottom of her skirt. One of the many souvenirs left over from their midnight race to the sanctuary. Arrows that had miraculously failed to hit their mark. Savaging her clothes instead of her skin.

"*Seven hells*," she swore quietly, giving it a useless tug. It was already three planks deep. She'd have to tear out almost everything she'd done.

There was a sound of light laughter as Rose sank beside her on the stone.

"You know, for a princess, you certainly have a colorful vocabulary. I can't imagine they condoned that kind of language back at the castle."

Katerina glanced at her quickly, then dropped her eyes back to the bridge. She hadn't spoken to the shifter since her secret had been revealed. Truth be told, she hadn't spoken with her since even longer than that. The two had fallen out before they'd ever really fallen in—sometime around the night when the little minx had made a play for Dylan Aires.

"Just tear it off."

Rose reached for the dress, but Katerina yanked it away.

"No—don't." The words rang out sharply between them, and she tempered her tone with a little sigh. "It's the only one I have. I can't just go ripping it to pieces."

The sky-blue silk fluttered lightly in the breeze, one corner pinned down beneath the planks of wood. Katerina remembered the day she'd gotten it. Rather, the day Dylan had stolen it for her.

"Of course, I stole it. You didn't think I actually went out and bought a dress, did you?"

Typical Dylan.

A strange emotion flashed through Rose's eyes before she shoved the princess' hands aside and took the end of the rope for herself.

"All right, then, we'll untangle it."

It was Katerina's turn to flash a look, but the two of them lapsed into silence. One of them sitting numbly with her hands on her knees. The other, unwinding the rope from the wood with a lot more skill than had been used to secure it in the first place.

Only five quiet minutes later, the last of the planks fell away and the dress sprang free. It fluttered lightly back to the princess' side, embarrassed to have caused so much trouble, as each girl finally forced themselves to look the other in the face.

"Thanks," Katerina mumbled, with a hint of a blush. "You're actually a lot better with those knots than most of us who work here. You should really think about—"

"I wanted to apologize," Rose interrupted with no preamble, "for that night at the bar. I had too much to drink, and probably said some things I shouldn't have. Granted, you strike me as super over-sensitive, and with the way those guys look, *someone* should be fucking them. But it wasn't my place to impose, I didn't want to overstep, and thus, my much-delayed apology. I'm...*sorry*."

She shuddered, as if the word had physically pained her to say, but then nodded decisively just after, like it was a job well done. Katerina raised her eyebrows and couldn't help but smile.

"You okay there? You look a little sick."

The shifter exhaled as if she'd just undergone a great trial.

"I'll breathe through it. People apologize every day. There are seldom fatalities."

The two shared a look, then burst into laughter. Laughter that quieted with just as sudden shyness. Two pairs of eyes shot in opposite directions as they sat there on the stone.

When Katerina got up that morning, she wouldn't have thought that 'shy' was anywhere in Rose's repertoire. But looking at her now—fidgeting fingers and nervous, sideways glances—it was easy to see the girl wasn't nearly as confident as she seemed. Beneath all that leather and aggressive sex appeal, she was just a teenager. A teenager armed with enough steel to singlehandedly take back the five kingdoms, but a teenager nonetheless.

"I've been here over a year," she said suddenly. "A whole year of just...nothing." Her eyes took on a wistfulness she didn't seem fully aware of herself. "You learn to content yourself with little things. To take in details. But it's a lot of staring out the window. Counting the chimes of the bell."

A sudden pang of sympathy tightened the princess' chest, and she felt her heart reaching out to the girl. Growing up in the castle, she knew exactly the feeling Rose had described. To have one's entire life reduced to a waiting game. Trapped in a permanent state of limbo. Unable to do anything but watch as the rest of the world went on without you. Your own life's story...passing you by.

Granted, the castle wasn't exactly the monastery. But in a strange way, the two were strikingly similar. In the end, it was just a different kind of cage.

"Yeah, I can understand that," she said quietly. The girl shot her a priceless look, and she laughed again. "Hey—you'd be surprised. The life of a princess isn't all it's cracked up to be. Just today, for example, I tied my only dress to a bridge."

The shifter lit up with a sudden smile. A smile that was a lot different than the ones Katerina had seen before. This one was unscripted. Relaxed in a way the others were not.

"Yeah, you're definitely not what I expected you to be." Rose shook her head thoughtfully, that smile still lingering on her face. "In fact, I'm having an unusually hard time figuring you out."

"What's there to figure out?" Katerina teased, giving the rope an extra tug as she threaded it through the first hole. "I'm a runaway princess who decided to take up construction and heights—"

"You're a Damaris on the run from the royal army, who won the allegiance of a shape-shifter, a wolf, and a fae." Rose's eyes twinkled as she held the board steady, picking up another as the princess tied the first knot. "So, your quirky new hobbies aside, *princess*, I think there's a little more to you than meets the eye."

Since running away from the castle and meeting her new band of friends, Katerina had made an unofficial study of the way people said the word. *Princess*.

Tanya said it merely as a place-holder. A word that could have easily been exchanged for any other as she demanded that Katerina surrender a larger share of the blankets or sample the latest disastrous attempt at cooking. Cassiel alternated, depending on his mood. At times, the title was a vile curse—as dark as one could imagine. At times, it was a sarcastic jab—a teasing reminder of that heavy crown and the weight that came along with it.

Dylan had his own way of saying the word. One that sent little shivers of anticipation up and down Katerina's spine. Whether it was a joke, a warning, or a whispered affirmation in the princess' ear, there was always more to it than met the eye. A layer of subtext, hiding just beneath the surface.

Katerina couldn't quite figure out how Rose said it. The word itself sounded strange coming out of her mouth. It was as though she was on the fence, waiting to be swayed either way.

"What happened to your hand?"

The moment passed, and the princess glanced down in surprise. She'd been frantically trying to come up with some brilliant existential answer for whatever truth Rose was trying to find. But the shifter didn't seem to require any sort of explanation. She just gestured to the princess' broken finger with a curious frown, picking up another plank of wood at the same time.

"Tell me you didn't rope that into the bridge, too."

"No," Katerina laughed, liking the girl more and more in spite of herself, "that was a left jab gone awry." Their eyes met, and she hastily explained. "I asked Cassiel to teach me how to fight."

"You did?" Rose looked genuinely surprised. Then impressed. "Well, that's a great idea. It kind of seems like everyone wants to kill you, right?" She gestured to the army with a casual nod of her head, then returned to the bridge. "Might as well do whatever you can to be prepared."

Katerina stared at her for a moment, then turned back to the rope with a smile.

Yeah, I like her. But I want to slap her at the same time.

"At any rate, I'd be happy to help if you ever need another sparring partner."

This time, the surprise was all Katerina's. It was strange enough that the two were sitting there having a frank conversation. Now she was offering to help?

"Really? You would?"

"Absolutely." The shifter twisted the rope around with a sudden grin. "Late-night workout sessions with a prince of the fae? Sweating it out with everybody's woodland wet dream?"

There it is.

The princess laughed aloud and returned to her work. It was easier to get past the incessant flirting, now that she saw how harmless it was. It was even possible to play along.

"I'm afraid you might be disappointed," she warned with a theatrical sigh. "Considering what a notorious womanizer that man is, he's surprisingly monogamous."

The girls shared a quick grin, but the shifter was already dreaming.

"You know what, Kat—you don't even need to come. I'll just tell you what happened at the end of every session. Give you my notes..."

She trailed off suddenly as the same shifter who'd instigated the fight with Dylan all those weeks ago made his way out onto the terrace. Thus far, Katerina and the others had been able to avoid him. He had classes in the first half of the day and trained in the other—so it hadn't been that hard. But it looked as though that luck had finally run out.

Sure enough, he took one look at the princess before making his way slowly across the wet stones. His usual band of followers was looming tall on every side.

Both Rose and Katerina pushed to their feet. Staring cautiously all the while.

"On second thought, maybe you should go to those sessions after all." Rose stuck her hands deep in her pockets. "It looks like you're going to need all the help you can get."

"Good morning," the shifter said as soon as he got close enough. Despite the casual aggression to his stance, his face was covered with a huge smile. One that showed every one of his teeth. "Getting to work early, I see."

"Well, you know what they say," Rose started as she took a step forward, incidentally angling the princess out of sight, "the early bird...does something. Idioms were never my strong suit."

The words fell on deaf ears, but the man pulled up short when he saw Rose. Clearly, he'd interpreted the lack of Katerina's three friends to mean the princess was essentially 'alone.' He hadn't imagined there might be someone else in her corner.

"Rose?" His pace slowed, and for the first time the men beside him faltered. "What're you doing here? I didn't know you were helping with the bridge."

"You know me," she smiled sweetly, "any chance for pre-dawn manual labor—I'm there."

"You know this creep?" Katerina muttered under her breath, wondering why she'd skipped breakfast and strayed so far away from the gang to begin with.

"We're in an alpine monastery." Rose's lips twitched up with a humorless smile. "Everyone knows everyone." She raised her voice, so the conversation included the newcomers as well. "Kat, this is Randall. Randall, I believe you already know my friend, Katerina."

Friend?

Katerina stifled her surprise and took great comfort in the word, coming to stand by her new friend's side. It was still six to two. One of whom had only recently learned not to tuck her thumb under in a fist but, regardless, the pack of shifters was forced to pause. They had no wish to harm one of their own. Especially one as volatile and temperamental as Rose.

"I didn't—" Randall hesitated, thrown off his game but unwilling to give up so easily. "I didn't realize the two of you were friends."

Neither did I.

A slender arm wrapped firmly around Katerina's shoulders. A gesture that was as friendly as it was a clear warning. Randal stopped his slow advance as those surrounding him took a step back.

"More like frenemies, but I think we took a big step today. Don't you, Kat?"

A wave of hysterical laughter bubbled up in Katerina's throat, and it took everything she had just to keep it together. Saying a word like 'frenemies' to a guy like Randall, especially in light of the present circumstances, seemed like throwing gas on the fire. But Rose somehow did it with a smile.

"What about you, Randall?" Her head tilted to the side, and all at once that sweet smile was as dangerous as it could be. "Are you *friends* with Katerina, too?"

The princess didn't know exactly how it happened. How the air seemed to chill and the gang of burly men in front of her shrank back at the words of one slender, smiling girl. But they did.

At the same time, the monastery bell chimed for morning classes to begin.

Randall's eyes flickered up to the clock tower as the doors to the sanctuary opened and the courtyard began flooding with people. The men standing around him melted away into the crowd until, at last, it was just the three of them standing there. None of them yet daring to move.

"Shouldn't you be getting to class, Rose?"

Randall tried to smile as well, but it simply looked as though he was baring his teeth. The princess stifled a shudder as her new friend stepped up to bat.

"Shouldn't you?" Her eyes danced as she cocked her head towards the main hall. "Tell you what, we can walk there together."

In a fluid movement, she left Katerina and wrapped her arm through Randall's at the same time. From a distance, it would look like nothing more than a friendly gesture. Only up close could Katerina see the amount of force she was using to keep him by her side.

"It's a date." He dipped his head in a gentlemanly sort of way before glancing over his shoulder at Katerina with a leer. "I'll be seeing you later, princess. Sometime when we can have a little more...privacy."

The word tickled her ear and Katerina seethed with rage as the two shifters vanished into the crowd. Never had she felt such unadulterated hatred of a single human being. Never had she truly understood the phrase, 'boils my blood.'

It was like there was an actual fire burning inside of her. Simmering deep inside her veins. Consuming her slowly from the ground up. It was only a matter of time before she lost control completely. Before the flames overtook her and there was nothing left to—

"Hey."

The princess shrieked aloud as a hand came down upon her shoulder. Her heart pounded like a hammer behind her eyes, and a furious blush was soon to follow when she looked up and saw Dylan staring down at her with concern.

"Are you okay?" He lifted his hand slowly off her skin. "You're burning up."

The debilitating rage slowly subsided as she struggled to catch her breath.

"What? Oh—I've been out here. Working." She gestured to the pile of planks and rope, shielding her eyes against the blinding sun, before looking up once more, suddenly on guard. "What do you want, Dylan? Because I don't care what you say, I'm meeting up with Cassiel tonight—"

"You're not going to spar with Cass anymore."

She blinked and stepped back in surprise. She'd expected him to sugarcoat it. To try to reason with her, or at least pretend as though she had a choice. She hadn't expected...*this*.

"Well, that's just—"

"Let me finish."

"No! This is complete bull! It's not up to you, Dylan—"

"Will you please just shut up?"

"*You* shut up! I'm sick and tired of putting up with your condescending, superior—"

A soft finger pressed over her lips as he looked down with a slightly frustrated smile. "You're not going to spar with Cass anymore...you're going to spar with me."

Chapter 10

For fifteen days, Katerina had been stranded at the monastery. Fifteen days of staring at the massive army beyond. At the strangers within. Fifteen days of pushing her mind and body as far as they were able to go. But never once, in all those days, had she found herself as frightened as she was now.

"Would you stop looking at me like that?" Dylan glanced over his shoulder as he lit the last of the candles. "You're making me feel like a monster."

Katerina hastily averted her eyes, standing awkwardly in the middle of the room. "Yeah. Sorry."

Shortly after the bell had rung for lights out, he'd come to her door and taken her to the same room where she'd been practicing with Cassiel. The same familiar room, but she suddenly felt as though she was standing in it for the very first time. The mats imprinted awkwardly under her feet. The air felt too warm. The mirrors reflected every glint of terror shining in her eyes.

This is a mistake. This is a huge mistake—

"First things first," Dylan announced, dropping the matches and coming to join her in the center of the floor. "You're going to want to take those clothes off."

Katerina blinked slowly, feeling every nerve ending on her body come to life. "...excuse me?"

With a little smile, he reached down and picked a small pile of clothing up off the mats. Next to it lay two small canteens of water, and a roll of gauze.

"You can't very well learn to fight in a dress, can you? Hardly appropriate." He handed the clothes to her with that same quirky grin. "Try these on. They looked to be about your size."

She accepted them robotically, staring down in shock. They were made of the same soft, worn fabric as most of his. A nondescript color somewhere between brown and grey. The kind that let you move freely and blend in, no matter where you were.

There was just one little problem...

"Pants?" Her eyes darted up in shock as the legs unrolled with a flourish in between them, tumbling to the floor. "I've never...I've never worn pants before."

It would have been unthinkable. Not even the castle maids would stoop so low. Katerina had seen an occasional peasant farmer or two donning slacks as she'd ridden through a village, but the concept of *pants* was simply not acceptable for a woman. And definitely not a princess.

That being said...Rose wore pants. Tight leather pants that clung to her legs and caught the eye of every man within a ten-foot radius. Maybe there was something to them after all. And if they let her move more easily? If they helped her fight?

"Well, there's a first time for everything." Dylan's eyes twinkled as he looked her up and down, apparently trying hard not to smile, or laugh. "I imagine the two of us are going to have a lot of firsts in this room."

What the heck is THAT supposed to mean?!

At this point, Katerina honestly didn't know what was flustering her more: The pants, the innuendoes, the candles, or the twinkle in his eyes. Cassiel was one of the most hands-down beautiful people she'd ever seen, and the first time they'd sparred he'd taken his shirt off. Not once in that entire night, or any night after, did she feel the way she did now.

Like at any moment, she might lose control. Like at any moment, he might let her.

"Do you mind?" She summoned enough of her wits to twirl her fingers expectantly in the air, gesturing for him to turn around. "Nice of you to give me these *here*, not in my room." *Where I could change behind a closed door.*

After all this time, she didn't have to see his face to imagine the mischief in his eyes.

"You know what—I completely forgot," he answered innocently. "But you're right. That would've given you a lot more privacy. My apologies, princess."

She bit down on her lip and turned around with a smile, pulling loose the ribbons that held her dress and letting the fabric fall to the floor. From the corner of her eye, she saw his entire body stiffen when he heard it land. She was naked. Just a few feet away. He was *very* aware of it.

But he was a good boy. He didn't turn around.

"Where did you get this?" she asked, stalling for time as she battled with the straps on the tunic. "Leftovers from your cross-dressing past?"

He chuckled, running his fingers through his hair. "I borrowed them from the laundress."

There was a pause.

"Borrowed?"

A much longer pause.

"...liberated."

I should start making a list. Of the clothes he's 'liberated' for me. This, the dress... what's next?

A few seconds later, the princess felt completely unrecognizable. The ruffles and royalty were put away. The delicate flower was placed on a shelf. She was a weathered traveler now. Ready for anything. A few shots of whiskey, and she might try passing herself off as a ranger for fun.

"Okay...I'm dressed."

Her crimson hair spun around her as she gave a self-satisfied twirl. For the first time in her life, ten bolts of fabric didn't twirl around to follow. She felt lighter. Free. Able to move and twist and bend in a way she'd never imagined possible. A little giggle escaped as she twirled again.

"I feel like I'm auditioning for a play." She held up the sleeves, looking down at herself with absolute delight. "Chimney sweep number five. Or maybe some kind of pirate—"

"All right, let's not get carried away." He pulled a leather cord from his wrist and swept back her hair, securing it in a gentle knot behind her head. She stared straight up at him, daring him to make eye contact, and he pursed his lips to restrain a smile. "You look adorable."

"*Fierce*," she corrected fervently. "I look *fierce*. Like a pirate."

"Okay, pirate." He took a step back onto the mats, casually raising his hands. "Let's see how fierce you can be."

Katerina felt her face pale as the reality of what was about to happen settled in hard. The thumb automatically tucked under. She forced herself to remove it. "You know what?" She fell back a step, tripping over the canteens in the process. "Maybe we should actually save this for a better—"

"*Hey.*" All at once he was standing right in front of her, gazing steadily into her eyes. "What are you so afraid of? It's just like working with Cassiel."

A rosy blush colored her cheeks, and she dropped her eyes to the mat. "...it's nothing like working with Cassiel." She slowly brought her eyes up to his chest, not daring to go further.

Even so quiet, the words had a profound effect. The room fell awkwardly silent as Dylan found himself suddenly unable to meet her gaze. But only a second later, he was collected and sure. "Maybe it'll be better?"

She lifted her eyes to see him staring down at her with a coaxing smile. A smile so boyish and charming and adorable it wasn't long before she found herself smiling, too. The second that she did, his face lit up and he beckoned her forward once more. Eyes dancing with anticipation.

"All right then, princess—er, pirate." Those hands of his were up again, ready and waiting. "Show me what you got..."

For a moment, they both stood there. Hands at the ready. Holding their breath.

Then, when it became clear nothing was going to happen, Katerina awkwardly cleared her throat. "...this is where Cassiel usually attacks me."

Dylan stared at her for a second, then he surprised her with a sudden laugh. As sweet as it was disarming. "I'm sure he does. The guy is direct." The princess nodded, bracing herself once more, but her opponent had no intention of moving. "But I want *you* to attack *me*."

Katerina froze, at a loss as to where to even begin, and he stepped forward patiently.

"Don't get me wrong, Kat. I want you to learn to *defend* yourself. This is about you being safe, not bold. The first move I want you to consider always is to run." His eyes shone with the gravity of what he was saying. "But the best way to prepare for an attack is to come at it from the other side. To put yourself in your attacker's shoes. That makes it predictable. That makes it a fight you'll know how to win. Now, think; whatever Cass showed you—use it on me. Attack."

For a moment, she considered. Then she took a deep breath and stepped forward.

Two-part combination. You got this.

With a skill and focus she hadn't possessed just two weeks before, Katerina flew fearlessly towards him and lashed out with her left hand. He dodged it gracefully, and she was in the process of throwing out her elbow to prepare for her kick, when all her movement came to a sudden halt.

"What—" She looked up in alarm, to find Dylan standing just inches away. He was holding her fist in one hand and her arm in the other. "I wasn't—"

"I'm guessing Cass always lets you finish the moves, since he wants you to learn them." Dylan nodded as though this was perfectly acceptable, then tightened his grip. "It's a good start, but it's not the way things will happen in a real fight. Now what would you do if I did this?"

Without a hint of warning he spun her around, slamming her back into his chest. She let out a gasp as a lock of her hair came loose. He was as graceful as he was strong. And the move reminded her strangely of something she'd see in a waltz. Something her dancing instructor would clap out on his wrist as she twirled across the floor.

Then his arms tightened around her chest, and she came back to the present.

"What are you going to do?" he asked quietly.

She ignored the way his breath tickled the back of her neck and tried to think. Cassiel had taught her how to flip someone over, but he was holding her too tightly for that. She could try to side-step away, but his boots had anchored hers into the floor.

"I haven't learned this yet—"

"This isn't about practiced movements," he interrupted gently. "It's about instinct. You can have all the lessons in the world, but nothing beats blind instinct when you find yourself in a fight."

Katerina froze for a moment, holding perfectly still. Then, with exaggerated slowness, she dug her elbow into the side of his ribs.

"That's right." She heard the pride in his voice and knew she had done well. "I'm wide open there, and it's a sensitive area. What else?"

Another pause. Then she tilted her head back until it was touching his.

"Do that hard enough—you'd break my nose. What else?"

One final pause, then she looped her foot behind his and turned around so the two were standing face to face. This time, she saw the pride firsthand. And the tender smile that went with it.

"That's right, princess." His arms tightened, and her heartbeat fluttered in her chest. "You have me standing here. What are you going to do next?"

She stared at him for a moment, losing herself deep in those beautiful eyes. Then she kicked him between the legs.

"SEVEN HELLS!"

The arms disappeared, and she sprang free, watching with a grim sort of satisfaction as he sank to his knees, head bowing towards the floor. Katerina of two weeks ago would have slapped herself across the face. Katerina of two months ago would have fainted dead away. But they were playing a different game now. The stakes had changed. And she had changed with them.

"I'd probably do something like that."

Dylan stayed down for a few seconds, the tips of his hair skimming the mats as he struggled to catch his breath. When he finally straightened up, a little stiffer than before, the smile was gone but the pride remained. In fact, the pride was even fiercer than before.

"And you'd probably win."

They were quiet for moment. Each staring at the other. Each feeling the subtle shift as the dynamic that had governed them before silently vanished.

Then Dylan lifted his hands and squared his jaw with determination.

"Again."

FOR THE NEXT FEW HOURS, the rest of the monastery slept while the ranger and the princess engaged in the battle of a century. Flying back and forth across the room. Lost in their own world.

After the first few times Dylan threw her into the floor, Katerina realized that he had no trouble being rough with her. And after the first few times she caught him off guard and struck him in the face, she realized she had no trouble being rough either.

It was like ripping off a bandage. One she'd never known was there.

She and Cassiel had been learning the basic moves. Mastering the essentials, so she could one day put them into practice. Dylan threw her straight into the deep end.

Any reservations she might have had that made her unsure of herself, any hesitation before charging straight into a fight, melted clean away as he forced her to do it again and again. The fear of the unknown vanished into thin air as he methodically took her through every possibility. Stripping away the hypotheticals. Getting right down to the gritty reality and letting her see it for herself.

Physically, it was an experience unlike anything she'd ever known. She'd been shaken by the avalanche. Stunned by the woods. She'd been fundamentally depleted by the midnight sprint that brought them to the monastery walls. But this was different. This was an actual *fight*. Fist by fist, bruise by bruise, she was learning something here. She was hurting, but she was rising above.

And she had never felt more alive.

"I still can't believe you kept this from me." Devon shifted his weight and moved slightly to the right.

The sun was just beginning to rise over the tips of the trees, but the two showed no signs of stopping. Quite the contrary. They were moving just as quickly as when they'd first begun.

Katerina opened her mouth to defend herself, but Dylan didn't give her the chance. In a move so fast she could hardly see, he grabbed her by the wrist and flipped her over onto the floor.

"Of all the things for you to keep a secret..."

All the air rushed out of her body with a broken gasp, and she pushed to her feet with a scowl. Blowing her hair out of her eyes, she raised her fists between them.

"In case you forget, peasant, I'm under no obligation to tell you how I spend my time." She moved as if to come at him from one angle, then ducked cleverly to the side. "This is a business arrangement, nothing more." A sharp punch to his ribs, which earned her a punishing blow to the back of the head. "At any rate, it's not like you tell me everything..."

"I tell you a lot," Dylan countered, jumping back to avoid a kick to the jaw. She raised her eyebrows slowly, hands on her hips, and he surrendered the point. "...I tell you more than most."

Another blur of limbs, from which both leapt away. Panting.

"You didn't tell me you slept with Cassiel's sister."

The fighting came to a momentary stop as he stepped back in surprise.

"...that was a long time ago." His chest rose with shallow, rapid breaths as he stared with wide eyes across the floor. "He told you that?"

"Yes, he did. Because, unlike you, *he* isn't shrouded in mystery." Katerina made her way to the side of the room and retrieved the canteens of water, tossing one to him and keeping the other for herself. "Although, to be honest, I wouldn't have thought that some breathtaking woodland princess would be your type. I happen to know firsthand that you tend to avoid enchanting royalty."

For a second, Dylan froze dead still. Every inch of his body going rigid all at once. Then he realized she was grinning, and his body relaxed with a tentative breath.

"That's right...dazzling women with a kingdom to their name? I hardly see the appeal."

Katerina's eyes flashed but her lips twitched upwards, playing along with the game. "Don't be hard on yourself," she replied casually. "We're not for everyone. No, I would guess your type would be more along the lines of something you'd find in a zoo. Feasts on raw meat by the light of the full moon. Slutty little thing. Creepy eyes..."

The smile melted off his face, and for a moment he was dead serious. "I told you. I'm not interested in Rose."

Katerina threw her canteen at his, knocking it clean out of his hand. "Who said anything about Rose?" For a second, the two just stood there. Then her eyes danced with sudden mischief. "But it's funny that her name would come to mind..."

She skipped backwards across the mats as he moved forward with a huge grin.

"Oh, you're so dead."

They collided a second later, falling to the floor in a tangle of laughter and limbs. Hands grabbed hands. Legs pinned each other to the ground. It went on for quite some time, growing more exhausted and ludicrous by the minute, until finally, in a massive show of strength, Dylan rolled on top—pinning her arms inescapably above her head.

It was here that they suddenly froze, the smiles still lingering on their faces. His dark hair tickled the sides of her face and she could almost hear the words. The same ones he'd been chanting at her the entire night.

You got me here, princess. Now what are you going to do?

She knew what she wanted to do. She knew it with every fiber of her being. But instead of acting on that impulse, her body relaxed with a quiet truth as she stared up into his eyes. "I missed you."

His grip loosened as his face lightened with surprise. Then uncertainty. Then some feeling Katerina was unable to place. He settled on sincere. "I missed you, too."

It wasn't until they said the words aloud that Katerina realized how true they were. When Dylan had caught her training the night before, he'd mentioned how he'd thought she was avoiding him. But, in hindsight, it was easy to see they'd been avoiding each other.

Since that fateful dawn where the monks had pulled them apart, there had been a distance between them. One that was hard to define. One that was impossible to ignore.

One that was chipping away at them, one piece at a time.

"I'm sorry," he whispered. For what exactly he was apologizing, Katerina wasn't sure. "Can we just...go back to the way things were before? Before they got so complicated?"

His breath washed over her face. His lips were hovering just an inch from hers. A shiver ran through her body as his hands tightened on her wrists. As he closed his eyes and leaned down—

"No."

She pulled back, her body turning to stone.

"We can't."

The next second, she rolled over, dropping him on the floor, and quickly stood. Leaving the practice room behind her. Moving furiously down the hall. In such a blind rage that she hadn't even remembered to take her dress with her. That she'd left without seeing the look on his face. Without giving him a chance to say goodbye.

The flames of the torches flickered as she stormed past, dimming to a low whisper, then springing back to life the second she was gone. One by one, they counted down the doors to the end of the hallway, until at last she was at her own.

Of course, that's exactly when Dylan caught up with her.

"Katerina, just listen—"

She didn't think. She shoved him hard into the wall.

"No! YOU listen!" Her eyes shone with tears, but the last thing she'd ever do was cry. "I told you I LOVE you, Dylan! I told you I LOVE you, and you WALKED AWAY! There is no coming back from that! It's OVER! It's DONE!"

The memory crushed her all over again, and she took a step back. Shaking from head to toe.

She sucked in a sharp breath. "A part of me wishes I'd never met you. That it wasn't you in that tavern. That it was someone else instead. Then this would be easier. Then I wouldn't feel like—" She cut herself off quickly, refusing to say another word. She had given enough of herself to this wasted fantasy of theirs. It was time to move on. "There is no going back," she repeated, quiet as a grave. "That was your decision, not mine."

The lights flickered once more as she pulled open her door, slipping safely inside.

"Don't ever try to kiss me again."

The world went dark as the door slammed between them. Leaving her with nothing but endless shadows. And a memory of that haunted look in his eyes.

Well, it's certainly over now.

She sank down where she stood, leaning against the wall as her body shook with silent, wracking sobs. She felt so alone. Never had she felt so hopeless and dejected than at this moment. She angled herself to the window and questioned the darkness, her hand held up in question, arms shaking. *Why?*

The man she loved was standing on the other side of that door. Frozen in place. Looking as if his entire world had come crashing down. And she, Katerina, was the one who'd crashed it.

But what else could I do? He doesn't love me back!

A wave of absolute, gut-wrenching agony coursed through her body as a flame of light suddenly shot into the night sky. Illuminating the darkness. Chasing those shadows away.

The world paused. Katerina slowly lifted her head.

...what?

The light had been real. Her eyes still burned from it. But where had it come from? She didn't have any candles lit. And her window faced west. It didn't catch the sunrise, and even if it could the sunrise didn't look like that.

It had been like a meteor. A flash of light. A streak of flames like...

Her mouth fell open and her face went pale.

...like the ones coming out of her hands?

Chapter 11

"What the...?"

When Katerina was little, she and her friends used to pretend they had superpowers. That they could use magic like all those fantastical creatures they read about in their stories. They would play for hours, shrieking with laughter as they ran through the trees. Wielding imaginary lightning bolts and fireballs. Flying high in the branches or melting invisibly into the underbrush. Summoning monsoons and changing into any number of frightening beasts.

The memories still brought tears of laughter to Katerina's eyes. Looking back, they were some of the best days of her life. Pretending she had a power that no one else could see.

But...this? This was nothing like that.

"*Shit*!" she cursed under her breath, staring in horror at the flames snaking around her wrists.

At any moment, she expected to scream in agony. For the paralyzing shock to give way and the unbearable burning pain to set in. But that never happened. Instead, she simply sat there. Staring with wide eyes as the golden coils twinkled innocently in the dark. Like a fiery, incandescent bracelet that was beautiful to look at, but she was unable to take off.

Unable to take off being the key phrase.

"Stop it!" she whispered frantically, beating her arms against the floor. "Go away!"

That's right, genius. Let's try talking to the fire. Maybe try stopping, dropping and rolling?

Her inner voice scorned and disowned her as she scrambled to the bed, thanking all the heavenly powers that Dylan had happened to tie back her hair. A second later, she ripped the sheets off the mattress—throwing them over one of her arms as the other beat at it with all her might.

For a second, it looked like it was working. There was a muffled hiss and a plume of smoke rose out from the center of the blanket.

"Okay...it's all okay." She about cried in relief, slowly extracting her arm so she could begin work on the other. "Everything's going to be okay."

That's when the blanket caught fire.

"What—no! No, no, no, no!"

The flames glistened and twinkled, mocking her as she jumped up and down on top of the smoldering fabric. She and her friends had done enough to strain the supplies of the monastery without setting the bedding on fire. And, given the royal army still sitting outside, the last thing she needed to explain was why there was a giant hole burned through the middle of her blanket.

Little bits of ash and singed cotton misted around her like an incriminating cloud, but she finally managed to put the flames out. The ones clinging to her arms were a different story.

"Why is this happening?!" She was so panicked, she found herself whispering aloud. Half expecting a voice to ring down from the heavens and answer. "Is this a prank?!"

Had that dark wizard decided to abandon his more concrete plans, giving in to basic trickery? Parlor games and mischief designed to wear down resistance and throw her off her game?

If that's the case...it's working.

As if to answer, the flames glowed even brighter. Sneakily lacing their way past her elbows as she stared on in dismay. Strangely enough, her tunic didn't catch fire. Neither did her new pants, although she was sure she must have brushed her arms against them half a dozen times.

STRANGELY enough? THAT'S what's strange here?!

"Okay, just think." She sat down in the middle of the floor, holding her arms out to her sides like a pair of flaming wings. "You're on fire. What puts out fire?"

It was a good thing the rest of the monastery was still asleep.

In the princess' own defense, it's incredibly hard to be discreet when half of your body is on fire. With all the subtlety of a rock through a window, she stole down the darkened hallways—casting the world's strangest shadows as she went—and poked her head out the door to the courtyard.

She was in luck.

The bell had yet to ring to wake people for morning prayers, and as far as she could see through the mist there was no one else out on the terrace.

Keeping her arms pinned awkwardly to her sides, as if that somehow hid the giant flames leaping off her skin, she sprinted across the damp stones toward the sanctuary, coming to a stop right in front of its imposing oak doors.

I mean no disrespect, she thought nervously, glancing up at the steeple. *This is strictly business.*

Then she plunged her arms deep into the prayer fountain splashing merrily by its doors.

Torrents of freezing water poured over her skin, soaking through her tunic in a matter of seconds. There were chunks of ice floating in the water. Ice that usually melted by the end of the day—but, given that it was shortly before dawn, the little fountain was still well below freezing.

Who cares if it freezes you. As long as it works!

Katerina closed her eyes, hardly daring to watch as she reached all the way to the bottom, pressing her palms against the icy tiles. If anyone dared to ask what she was doing, she'd say she was stealing coins. Looking for fish. Communing with the water nymphs.

Anything was better than the alternative. Anything was better than, 'Oh, funny you should ask! My body just burst into spontaneous flames and I'm trying to put them out before I burn this whole monastery to the ground. Not that the inhabitants could possibly escape. Since my friends and I already destroyed that handy bridge in and out of the place...'

"Please," she whispered, bowing her head like a prayer. "Please be gone."

She opened one eye. Then the other. Then let out a stifled shriek as those incorrigible flames twinkled back at her. Rippling at the bottom of the fountain like underwater jewels.

"Oh, dear, I see someone's having a rough morning."

Katerina whipped around with a gasp, flinging an arc of freezing water droplets, only to see Michael standing behind her. Hands folded neatly in front of him. Head bowed with a patient smile.

"I didn't...I mean, I wasn't..." A look of childlike guilt flushed across her face as she rather uselessly hid her arms behind her back. "...I was looking for fish."

In hindsight, she could only imagine how it must have looked.

The sanctuary doors framed in the background. Her cheeks as red as her hair. Her tunic dripping down her freshly-stolen men's pants. And then, of course, there were those pesky flames. Peeking out from behind her, like an ironic halo that refused to go away.

Michael's eyes twinkled, but he didn't smile. Instead, he merely cocked his head towards the main building. So casual, you'd think he found deranged pyromaniacs trolling the church fountain every day. "Did you ever get a chance to see the library, like I suggested?"

Katerina blinked as another flame curled discreetly up her shoulder. Here she was, a walking bonfire, and he wanted her to step inside a room full of books? Was the man certifiable? Or did he just have a secret affinity for property destruction?

"Uh...no. I didn't." She tried desperately to act as normal as him, flinching slightly as that same determined flame tickled at the side of her ear. "Not yet. But I will. It sounds lovely—"

"*Katerina*."

She stopped shivering and stammering long enough to listen. "Yes?"

This time, he couldn't help but smile. "You seem to be having a bit of an... issue. Why don't we step into my office?"

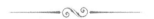

IN THE LAST TWO MONTHS, since she'd left the castle, Katerina had faced her share of what the rest of the world would call 'dangerous' people. From the assassins who chased her out of the castle, to the vampires determined to drain her at the bar. From the giant, to the soldiers, to the shifters, to the spirit of a dead fae queen out for blood. The list went on and on, right down to the seemingly sweet village hag who offered to buy one of her eyes. Truth be told, her own friends, her gallant protectors, were probably some of the most dangerous ones of all. Given their interesting backgrounds, she was sure the world would spare them no judgement.

But in all that time, she'd never met anyone who put her on notice like Michael.

There was something quite otherworldly about him. This coming from a girl who'd recently made some leaps and bounds into the realm of the supernatural. Something that went above and beyond anything she'd ever seen. And it wasn't just the fact that she felt as though he'd been around for as long as the mountain upon which he lived. It wasn't the fact that she'd never—not for a single second—understood the reason behind his intentions. It was something more than that.

It was his aura. The very essence of him as a person. He looked like a man but wasn't. He looked like he was fifty years old but wasn't. She wasn't quite sure what he was.

Perhaps she could have taken a cue from his office.

As the two slipped through a stone doorway carved into the wall of the sanctuary Katerina came to a sudden stop, staring around with wide eyes as she tucked her flaming arms carefully into the folds of her cloak. The office itself was simple. Desk, chair, modest window. It was the walls that caught her attention. The collage of brightly colored finger-paintings that covered the walls. Not an inch was spared. It was as though some kindergarten class had made the place their holy mission.

"Did you...paint these yourself?"

Probably best to break the ice. Start with a joke. Then we'll talk about the fact that my hands are on fire...

Michael shut the door, glanced over his shoulder in surprise, then burst out laughing. With the stately air of a headmaster or priest, he settled himself behind the desk and gestured for her to take the other seat. She did so hesitantly, keeping her arms carefully elevated above the wood.

"I've been working on them for years."

The princess blinked, realized he was joking, then forced a quick smile. This was her ice-breaking strategy, after all. It was best to play along.

"No, the children of the local villages make these for me." He pushed to his feet again and peeled the closest one off the wall. "Their first act of entry into Talsing."

"Their first act of entry?"

Katerina frowned in confusion, then reached out to examine the painting for herself. She remembered the fire a second later, blushed, then read from afar as he flipped it over.

The front may have been a child's painting, but the back was a different story. It was a cry for deliverance. Plain and simple. Written in a parent's worried hand.

Michael,

We beseech you to take Sarah, age five, under your guiding hand. She is a sweet girl with promise and potential but has attracted the kind of attention from which her mother and I are no longer able to protect her. Any help you could give would be forever appreciated. We will send funds as soon as available. A thousand thanks.

They didn't sign their names. Whether that was because they were worried the letter would be intercepted, or because they simply couldn't force the signature to send their daughter away, the princess would never know.

Her eyes lifted slowly to the hundreds of other paintings all over the office. Imagining the tear-stained words and pleas for sanctuary written on the other side.

"They're all the same?" she asked quietly, forgetting for a moment that she was on fire.

Michael nodded briskly, pinning the letter back in its place on the wall.

"Every one of them. Usually, not a month goes by when a child doesn't knock on the door to the monastery, searching for salvation. But the weather has been unusually cold, and we haven't had a new arrival for some time."

Attracted the kind of attention from which her mother and I are no longer able to protect her.

Katerina's lips parted as two and two suddenly clicked. "These children. They're all magical, aren't they? Gifted with supernatural abilities?"

It reminded her of something Tanya had said that night after they'd been drinking in the tavern. How a great deal of youngsters had been sent away from home for protection in sanctuaries like Talsing. Sent away by parents willing to do anything to keep them off the royal radar.

"Most of them, yes." Michael nodded curtly, sinking back down into his chair. "We get a few from time to time whose parents simply cannot afford to feed them."

A sudden image of a castle tea party flashed through Katerina's head. They had them every other Sunday. Tables laden with food so rich and decadent, the guests never made it through a single platter. Most of it got thrown away.

"And these parents...they send you funds?"

Again, Michael shook his head, continuing in his quiet, gentle manner. "Never. Even if they tried, we would never accept them. The safety of the children is our top priority. It's the main reason we need to repair the bridge. As of now, they have no way to get to us."

Katerina's face paled as her skin went cold. That morning, her own problems had seemed insurmountable. But faced with this tragic new wealth of information, they paled in comparison. At least she wasn't starving. At least she didn't have a starving child. "We're working on that as quickly as possible, I promise, but what are we going to do once it's finished?" The image of a little girl, stranded and alone on the wrong side of the mountains, burned into her very soul. Stealing her breath and trembling her hands. "Even if we can get the army to leave, we have no way to hang it! It's not like we can just carry it to the other side—"

"The army will leave eventually," Michael interrupted calmly. "And you just worry about building the bridge. When it's ready, I'll hang it myself."

"But how?" Katerina demanded, refusing to be reassured. All those happy finger-paintings were glaring down at her. A hundred pairs of eyes she would never see. "Dylan said that, you said that, everyone keeps saying to take that kind of thing on faith. But this is serious! You said it yourself: those kids need to get over here. How are you supposed to—"

A gust of wind hit her right in the face. Followed by something softer. Something that felt like the whisper-light touch of—

"...feathers." She stared up with wide unblinking eyes at the man standing before her. The exact same man who'd been speaking to her a moment before, except for one little difference.

The giant pair of wings that had sprung from his shoulders.

"You have...you have wings."

An astute observation. Dylan would have made a sarcastic joke. But it was all Katerina could do to string together a complete sentence. How was it possible to live in a world where these kinds of things kept happening? Where your friends turned into three-foot goblins, or savage forest beasts, or even something that looked disturbingly like a casually-dressed angel.

"...and I thought it was strange that my arms were on fire..."

Michael stared down kindly, and all at once the wings disappeared.

"Fire?" He cocked his head to the side, eyes twinkling in the morning light. "What fire?"

"HOW IS IT POSSIBLE?"

Katerina raced to keep up with Michael's long strides, scampering two steps for every one of his. The torches flickered beside them as they swept down the long corridors, but there were already people afoot whose job it was to put them out. Dawn had arrived. The endless night was over.

"Just tell me how it's possible," she begged again, tripping slightly as he came to a stop and started fiddling with the knob on a large arched door. "One second, I was trying to drown myself in the fountain so I wouldn't burn the monastery down, and the next—"

"You'll soon know how it's possible," Michael reassured her for the millionth time, pulling on the brass handle and stepping back to let her inside. "Patience, child. All will be revealed."

She swept past him, impatiently drumming her new flameless fingers against the sides of her pants, and then, for the second time in less than an hour, she froze to a complete stop. Her eyes widened as they adjusted to the softer lighting and she rotated in a slow circle as she gazed around the room. If you could even call it a room. The thing was like something you'd see in a fairytale.

Row upon row of ancient parchments. Level upon level of leather-bound books. They were stacked from the floor to the ceiling. And, given the monastery's unique architecture, that domed ceiling stretched all the way to the sky. A wheeled ladder had been fashioned to allow one to spin about in a circle as they searched for what they wanted, but even the ladder didn't begin to cover it.

I suppose when Michael wants a book that's too high on the shelves, he can just fly up to grab it.

Katerina's lips fell open and she turned around to see him silently reveling in her awestruck reaction. Michael might love the monastery, but this library was his pride and joy.

"It's incredible." She spoke before he could even ask the question, rotating in a slow circle to take it in all over again. There were books on every subject you could possibly imagine. From botany to mythology. History to science. Bohemian poetry to the technicalities of building a ship.

"It's exactly what *you* need."

Katerina glanced back in surprise. "What I *need*?" She loved the idea of the library, but unless there was a tell-all book about extinguishing one's own arms she didn't see how it would help her. "What do I *need* in the library?"

With a steady smile, Michael paced forward and extracted a piece of parchment from its place on the shelves. It was so old that half the letters had faded almost completely off the page, but Katerina was still able to make out the heading. A single name, written in slender, looping script.

Adelaide Gray

The princess' fingers tightened on the paper, tracing the edges as if it were the most precious thing in the world. She didn't know how long she stood there. She had all but stopped breathing by the time Michael placed a gentle hand on her shoulder.

"Answers," he replied quietly. "That's what you need from the library. Answers."

He swept out the door without another word. Leaving her standing in the middle of the floor. Pausing only to glance over his shoulder with a little smile. "I'll be back in a few hours. Take all the time you need."

Chapter 12

When Katerina first saw the parchment, she expected something like a personnel file. One of those dossiers the castle used to keep track of everyone. But what Michael handed her read more like a diary. A rain-soaked, tear-stained, ink-smeared diary. She wondered how it had possibly ended up in his hands. This was her mom. *Her* mom.

For the next few hours, she soaked up every bit of information she could find. Reveling in the mere sight of her mother's handwriting. Trying to decipher water-damaged words, most of them so lost to the ravages of time that they were beyond help. But there were a few entries that remained perfectly clear. One of them stood out to Katerina.

January 11,

I almost did the unthinkable today. I almost told Marcus. I wasn't planning on it. We were sitting down for lunch, the same as we do every day. But the twins had gone down for an early nap, so for the first time in a long while the two of us were alone.

I almost told him.

Staring across the table, I could imagine myself telling him. I could imagine the utter relief I would feel. The unspeakable joy of not having to carry this secret alone. He was my husband, my king. At one point, he had even been my friend.

Surely, he wouldn't turn me away like the others. Surely, he would understand.

Then Sir Lansbury walked in and announced they'd caught two renegade shifters attempting to flee the border. They were being dragged to the dungeons that very minute.

I looked at Marcus. Looked for any bit of empathy. Any trace of the man I had married still lingering in his eyes. But there was nothing.

That man is gone. And this secret is mine alone to keep.

The edges of the paper were singed, as if they'd been held too close to a fire. Katerina stared at them as a host of tears sprang to her eyes. As that secret of her mother's became hers to share.

Adelaide Gray was a supernatural. A shifter. As her daughter... does that make me a shifter, too?

The door opened and closed behind Kat, but the princess didn't need to look up to see who it was. This was his library, after all. And he'd read that parchment long before she had.

"She never said what she shifts into..." Katerina whispered faintly, speaking as though in a daze. The question occurred to her for the first time as she looked up into Michael's eyes.

He nodded thoughtfully and settled himself at the end of the table. "Maybe she didn't yet know. It's clear there were no others like her. She hid it very, very well. Whatever it was, it was powerful. She didn't even need to shift before starting to tap into its magic."

Katerina looked slowly from the parchment to her own trembling hands. He nodded again.

"Yes, my dear. Those beautiful flames. The ones you were trying so hard to hide. That's your mother's magic flowing through you. It's a part of who you are. It's in your blood."

For a split second, she didn't want it to be. For a split second, she felt a stab of that blind panic that her mother had to have been feeling every day. The feeling of being trapped in one's own body. A helpless prisoner to forces too powerful to escape. Too dangerous to control.

"You put them out yourself, you know." Her head jerked up again, and she saw Michael staring at her with a kind smile. "They vanished the second you were sufficiently distracted by the needs of others. It's why I brought you to my office. It's why I showed you those finger-paintings."

The simple logic of the plan slowly dawned on her, but the larger points remained vague.

"But how did you know that would happen?" she whispered, tucking her thumbs under as she curled her fingers into fists. Frightened that, at any moment, the whole nightmare might start up again. "I didn't know myself. I don't even know how they got started—"

"Every shifter is different," Michael interrupted gently. "But the laws that govern them are fundamentally the same. Your magic is connected to your emotion. For better or for worse. It's a thin line, but it's one you can learn to control."

Katerina flashed him a dubious look, and he chuckled softly.

"Think about it. What were you doing the first time the flames appeared?"

Her face flushed as she thought back to the night of sparring with Dylan. To the moment he'd tried to kiss her, and her fierce rejection as she pulled away. To the way her heart felt like it was breaking inside her chest as she sank to the other side of the door. Knowing that she'd just closed it forever. Knowing that the future she wanted so badly was never meant to be.

So that's the key? I just need to be blindingly, unspeakably sad to make these powers work?

Her heart flinched preemptively in her chest.

...sounds awesome.

But even as she thought the words, she realized they weren't true. The first time she'd felt the fire hadn't been with Dylan. She'd felt it building up in her hands when she wanted to fight Randall. Consuming her from the ground up. And even earlier—when she and Cassiel were banging on the sanctuary door. Her eyes widened as she remembered the shower of sparks when she struck the metal. She'd attributed it to a trick of the light. Maybe it was something more.

But I can't control it. Her whirlwind of chaotic thoughts ended with a simple, but inescapable truth. *It's just another way I'm going to hurt the people around me. The ones trying to keep me safe.*

"This isn't a curse."

Michael might have been a shifter himself, but Katerina could swear the man could read minds as well. No sooner had that hopeless despair settled over her than he got up from his chair and moved forward to take her hand.

"It is a *gift*."

Katerina's eyes watered, and for a fleeting moment a part of her dared to hope. But that moment passed, and she pulled away with a quiet sob. "No, it isn't. Maybe it's supposed to be, but mine isn't. Just look at what it did to my mother. Just look at what it's already doing to me. I could've burned this monastery down. I could have hurt anyone who came too close—"

"That's because it's brand new, child." Michael's eyes softened, and he stared at her with a lifetime's worth of patience. "Do you think Dylan knew how to turn into a wolf when he came to our gates? Do you think he could control it? The first time he grew claws, I thought the poor kid was going to have a heart attack." He chuckled quietly at the memory before leaning forward to take Katerina's hand once more. "But he learned. He'd been learning for years without realizing it before he came to the sanctuary, and he continued learning for years after he left. You will learn, too, child. I promise. This isn't the nightmare you fear. You see? I'm not afraid to touch you."

She looked down at their connection with a self-pitying sniff but took very little comfort in it. She imagined it would take quite a lot to make a man like Michael afraid.

He chuckled again and walked back to his seat. "I can see already you're going to be just as stubborn as he was. No doubt there will be many trips to the fountain by the time you're through."

She felt herself blush, but for the first time Katerina also felt a glimmer of something she thought had vanished the second she saw the flames. Hope.

"You really think that will happen?" she asked softly. "That there will be a time when I can control it? When I'm through?" She stared up at the man in earnest, laying every card and quiet vulnerability she had on the table. "This place can help me do that?"

Michael stared at her intently, as if there was a bigger picture she had yet to find. As if she'd stumbled onto the ultimate question without realizing it herself. "This is a place people come for guidance. For clarity." He spoke slowly, weighing each word before letting it go. "But the answers you seek? The magic you hope to control? That's something you brought with you. It's something you've always had."

KATERINA LEFT THE LIBRARY with a single thought on her mind. One that had been stuck on a loop ever since she'd picked up the parchment. Growing stronger and stronger with each moment.

Dylan...I have to tell Dylan.

It didn't matter that she'd been up training through the entire night. It didn't matter that her clothes were still soaked from her impromptu dive into the prayer fountain. It didn't even matter that their epic sparring session had ended in heartbreak and tears.

From the second she found out there was magic inside her, there was only one person in the entire world that she wanted to tell. That she *needed* to tell. She couldn't wait a second longer.

Unfortunately, there was a maze of unfamiliar corridors to get through first. And within a matter of seconds the princess was hopelessly lost.

"Son of a harpy!" she cursed and made the same turn she could swear she'd already made half a dozen times before, coming to stop beneath a suspiciously familiar painting of the Black Forest. She should have just asked Michael to walk her back to the courtyard, but she'd left in a rush, and after revealing that one has some great and unknown power lying inside them it's probably best not to follow it up with, 'That may be true, but I still can't find my way outside. Care for a walking buddy?'

A few more seconds of wandering and she found herself right back where she started, in the hallway outside Michael's office. She was about to give up altogether and knock on his door for help, when the door opened and the last person she'd expected to see slipped out into the hall.

"Tanya?"

The shape-shifter whirled around in surprise. Surprise that tripled when she saw the princess standing there. Soaking wet. Leaving a trail of sooty water in her wake. "Kat, what are you doing here?"

An echo of her rather strange morning flashed through her head, and the princess felt the sudden need to deny. "Me? Oh, nothing. Just stretching my legs a little before—"

"You're lost, aren't you?"

"...no."

The shifter pursed her lips, then cocked her head in the opposite direction back down the hall. Katerina lifted her chin and followed silently along, refusing to give anything away. Just three short minutes later—plus two doors Katerina would swear weren't there just moments before—and the two were back in the courtyard, squinting into the afternoon sun.

It was only once they were there, staring out over the magnificent vista, that the princess realized the obvious question. One she'd completely failed to connect just moments before.

"What were you doing in Michael's office?"

Tanya froze dead still, caught red-handed with no way to deny it. At first, it looked as though she might try anyway. But she gave up before she started, bowing her head with a defeated little sigh.

"I've been working with him." The princess shot her a questioning look, and she forced herself to continue. "He's been helping me. Ever since that day in the forest, the day I grew those wings...I didn't know I could do that." Her eyes warmed at the very thought of it before cooling suddenly. "I haven't been able to do it since."

Katerina's mouth fell open in shock. In the last few weeks, there had been several major life events that had fallen through the cracks. Collateral damage of living on adrenaline, running for their lives. But Katerina remembered all too well the moment her lovely friend had sprouted a pair of life-saving wings. In fact, she had the sudden suspicion she'd seen the same wings just hours before. "You and Michael...you've been training?"

It was the last thing in the world she would have expected, but in a way it made perfect sense. Tanya Oberon wasn't the kind of person to waste an opportunity. As long as they were trapped in a monastery with a mysterious magical guru calling the shots, she'd take full advantage.

Tanya blushed a delicate shade of pink, one that made her look surprisingly fragile in spite of the jagged mohawk tumbling down her back. "He and I have similar gifts. I know that the bridge is the top priority and everything, but now that my leg is better I was hoping he could help me—"

"Holy hot cakes!" Katerina exclaimed, looking down at the shifter's knee. "Your cast is gone!"

Tanya studied her for a moment before shaking her head with a slow smile. "Jokes aside, you are seriously one of the least observant people I've ever met."

"I'm just saying—"

"Yeah," Tanya grinned, "the cast is gone. I got it off a couple days ago."

"How is that possible?" Katerina frowned at the brace around her knee, as if she could see through it to the muscles and tendons below. "That was a horrible break, Tan. After Dylan pulled you out of the snow, we could see the bone..."

She shuddered at the very memory, but Tanya shrugged dismissively.

"Shifters heal a lot faster than people—we're wired differently. So are fae." She shot the princess another teasing grin. "That's why it's a good thing *you* didn't get all that hurt during the journey, you delicate little flower. We never would have made it to the monastery in time."

Shifters heal a lot faster than people—we're wired differently. Katerina looked down at her broken finger. A finger that was broken no more. *Dylan...I have to tell Dylan.* "Hey, do you know where Dylan is?" she asked quickly, ignoring Tanya's teasing jab as she glanced around the courtyard, like he might be lurking in the shadows. "I really need to talk to him."

"Dylan?" Tanya followed her gaze for a moment, slowly turning back around, her eyes tight with an emotion the princess didn't understand. "It's too late for that."

Katerina stopped her roving search at once, pulse quickening in her chest. "What do you mean it's too late? Where is he?"

Tanya stared at her for another moment. Before looking over the side of the mountain. "He's gone."

DYLAN AND CASSIEL HAD been warning the girls they'd be leaving to replenish the monastery's supplies. They'd been planning the expedition for days. Rose Macado, little instigator that she was, delighted in reminding the others of it every chance she got.

So, Katerina had no idea why she was so surprised when it finally happened.

"—just don't see how you could let them go off without us," she raged, gripping the edge of the northern most wall as she glared over the cliff. "And today of all days..."

Tanya rolled her eyes. She was as wound up as the princess but had a slightly more mature way of showing it. Or...less mature. Depending on how you interpreted the flask in her hand. "First off, I didn't *let* them go off anywhere. They set out before the sun came up; I didn't know it was happening." She took another swig, ignoring the burning taste that followed. "And second—what the hell is that supposed to mean? Today of all days. Today is just like any other."

Except that today I found out I'm a fire wielding shifter. Katerina's face paled with sudden horror. *And last night Dylan didn't get a wink of sleep.* She shook her head. "Isn't there a way we can get in contact with them?" she asked, standing on her tiptoes as she stared down the jagged mountain cliff. "We could send a raven, or...or maybe we could use the seeing stone again. They've already been gone for almost five hours; what if something's wrong—"

"*Hey,*" Tanya said, grabbing her firmly by the shoulders, "you know there's no way we can check in on them without alerting the enemy to their position, and you also know that, of all the people in the world, our guys know how to take care of themselves."

An image of Dylan and Cassiel fearlessly facing down the royal army flashed through her head, and Katerina nodded with a begrudging, "Yeah, I guess."

Tanya snorted, holding out the flask. "In the meantime, I say this as a friend: Drink."

The princess did as she was instructed, gulping down the burning liquid with a wince.

"That's the spirit." The shifter took back the flask with a smile. "Hey, look on the bright side—Rose is with them. Maybe she'll fall into the ravine or get eaten by a bear or something."

Katerina laughed shortly, feeling considerably better as the whiskey warmed her blood. "You know...she's actually not all that bad. Rose, I mean. I think she might be one of the good ones."

Tanya looked at her doubtfully. "The last time we talked, you said her eyes were fake."

The princess blushed. "...I wasn't myself."

For the rest of the afternoon the two girls stood on the highest parapet, scanning the mountain below for any sign of their friends. A band of other shifters had gone along with them, shifters who had friends back at Talsing, and it wasn't long before a little crowd joined their cause.

Minutes stretched into hours. Hours stretched into what felt like years. The sun was starting to drop behind the trees, tinting the sky a vibrant shade of gold, and all of Talsing had come out to wait.

"You know...Cassiel better have brought me back some kind of present."

Katerina turned to Tanya in surprise. The two of them hadn't spoken in quite some time, each lost to their own worried little trance as they gazed blankly into the trees. "A present?"

The shifter nodded soundly, as if it was the most obvious thing in the world. "For our anniversary. We've been together a month as of today."

Katerina's first reaction was surprise. Her second was straight-up confusion. "A month?" she repeated. "It hasn't been nearly a month. The first time you guys hooked up wasn't until the night after we woke up here at Talsing—"

"Yes, *technically*." Tanya nodded patiently. "But that's not how you judge anniversaries. I'm going from the first time I ever undressed him in my mind."

Worried as she was, the princess couldn't help but laugh. Of course, that's the way Tanya chose to commemorate their relationship. Not that Cassiel would have any idea that was the case...

"You know," she advised softly, "you might want to give him a word of warning. It isn't fair for you to expect the guy to have guessed what was going on inside your—"

A sudden flicker of light caught her eye. The glint of the setting sun against metal. Tanya saw it, too. They stopped talking at once and peered intently over the side. Searching for any sign of their friends. Any clue that the mission had been a success and they were on their way home.

...it came in the form of a scream.

"Run!"

There was a collective gasp from those gathered on the wall as a bloodied figure stumbled out of the trees. He was followed by five more after that. One of them wasn't moving.

"What's happening??" Katerina tried to shriek, but it came out as a whisper instead. Her nails dug into the stone railing, splintering to little shards as she gazed desperately over the edge. Trying to make out individual faces. Trying to spot her friends amongst the crowd. "What..."

A second later, she saw them. The reason for all the blood. The reason for all the haste. Six people had set out from the monastery that morning. Five shifters and one fae—each one more than capable of evading the royal army. Each one more than capable of taking care of themselves.

But they had discovered a hidden secret for which none of them could have been prepared.

...the royal army had shifters of its own.

"RUN!"

The voice shouted again, louder this time, and Katerina was able to see who it was. It was Randall—of all people. The permanent look of arrogance on the shifter's face had been replaced with one of abject fear. A second later, that face went blank as a knife was lodged in the side of his neck.

There was another scream, this time from right beside her, as the people of Talsing came alive. Shouting and crying for their friends to hurry. Beating uselessly against the wall with their hands. Throwing stones and pieces of plywood—whatever they could do to help, though they were far out of range. Yelling for Michael. Always for Michael. Where was he??

A second later, a giant shadow fell over the crowd.

Katerina looked up with the others to see a gigantic eagle soaring over top of them. An eagle the size of ten grown men. It swooped down towards the bloody field, lethal talons outstretched, and a second later it lifted one of the Talsing shifters into the air.

The princess looked on in horror, but the crowd gasped in relief. Then she understood.

Michael.

Talsing's sacred guardian did nothing to attack, merely to protect. With a mighty swoop of its wings, the eagle dropped the shifter safely inside the sanctuary walls and went back for another, but it was clear to see they were running out of time. Already, the shifters from the army were closing rank, and the Talsing warriors were running out of time.

"Tanya, we've got to—"

Katerina grabbed for her hand, but Tanya was already gone.

With a fearsome shout the girl threw herself over the edge of the cliff, sprouting wings herself as she swooped down into the field of battle. She nearly collided with a tall blond figure, who almost fell over in surprise, but a second later they were fighting side by side.

Well, that's one way to advance your powers. Just spike that adrenaline through the roof.

The sound of steel on steel echoed through the air. Across the mountain peaks, there was a distant roar—like an unruly sea. The army was cheering their people on, screaming for blood. Every few minutes, one of the men on both sides would disappear into a pile of clothes, and a raging wolf would spring up in his place. Biting and tearing. Going in for the kill.

Talsing was fighting bravely, but it wasn't enough. And still, Katerina had yet to find—

Dylan.

Her eyes locked onto him across the field. Somehow seeing every detail, despite the great distance between them. He was sprinting back up to the monastery, feet flying across the grass with every bit of strength he had. But he was falling behind. And he still hadn't shifted.

A second later, Katerina saw why.

It was Rose. The person who wasn't moving when they burst through the trees. The person who was currently flung across Dylan's back, slowing him down, risking his life. It was Rose.

...No!

Wolves were closing in from all sides. Tearing at his flesh. Ripping at his clothes. He was trying to fight them off as best he could, but there was only so much he could do with a body slung over his shoulder. He worked with his knife, one-handed, and never broke his stride. But it still wasn't going to be enough. More of the army's shifters were appearing every moment, and there was only a brief window of opportunity to get back to Talsing alive. A window that was closing fast.

Not if I can help it...

Looking back, Katerina didn't know what made her do it. Didn't know what instinct it was that propelled her forward. One second, she was standing there. Wringing her hands helplessly. Trying not to cry as the love of her life fought for his own. The next, she was climbing up a crooked set of steps, not stopping until she'd gotten to Dylan's old spot on the highest tower.

The wind picked up as she stepped out onto the ledge, lifting her hands into the air. "Take cover!" she screamed.

Dylan looked up the second he heard her voice. Right as the first flames started dancing in her hands.

Cassiel and Tanya looked up a second later, freezing in momentary shock.

For a moment, all was quiet. An unnatural hush fell over the people of Talsing and the soldiers waiting on the other side of the cliff. Even the eagle seemed to be holding its breath.

Then Katerina Damaris let loose a wave of fire the likes of which the world had never seen.

Chapter 13

The strange thing about dreams is you play by a different set of rules. The landscape may look the same, but the players are different. You instinctively understand the subtle shift. You instinctively know what's possible, and what's not. What you're capable of, and what you aren't.

Poised upon that stone ledge, her flaming arms stretched up to the sky, Katerina suddenly realized there weren't many things in the world that were beyond her reach.

A literal ocean of fire swept over the battlefield. Streaming from her hands. Sparking in her eyes. Hitting her targets with deadly precision, while sparing the lives of her friends. There was a sound of distant screams as the royal shifters who were still able fell back towards the forest. A whispered hush fell over the monastery, while the army on the other side was dead quiet.

Across the distance that divided them, Katerina imagined she could see Dylan's face. The way his lips parted in shock as the first wisps of golden fire lashed the air by his side. The way his blue eyes widened in wonder as they made the slow journey back to the girl standing on the ledge.

Then all was lost to smoke.

The battle was effectively over. The shifters of Talsing were racing back, unchallenged, to the monastery gate. The shifters of the royal army were fleeing for their lives, back to the woods.

The fight was finished, but Katerina was not. The wind stirred her crimson hair into a fiery cloud as her eyes locked upon each of the retreating warriors. The ones who had done her friends so much harm. The ones who would not live to see another sunrise.

Waves of hate welled up inside her, stronger than anything she'd ever known. Burning in her veins. Rushing down her slender arms before pouring from her palms into the world beyond. The screams of the royal shifters grew more and more desperate. Parts of the mountain had started to catch on fire. The flames danced in Katerina's eyes as she took down one after another. Delighting in the way their feeble bodies crumbled beneath her open hand. Reveling in each tortured cry before savoring the chilled silence that followed. *How dare they try to hurt my friends! They were going to kill Dylan! NEVER!*

It was a power unlike anything she'd ever known. Her first taste, but she was suddenly certain she could never be without it. Suddenly certain she could never get enough.

Why stop with the shifters? Her head tilted almost lazily to the side as she brought her hands together, doubling the blinding burst of fire. *Why not turn to the other mountain? To the army waiting on the other side? Doesn't matter how many people there are, they all want me dead. Why not end this right here and—*

"Katerina."

The fire disappeared as she turned around with a startled gasp. She'd been so intent on her murderous prize, she hadn't even seen the massive eagle fly up behind her. Disappearing in a whirl of feathers to reveal the solemn figure of a man.

"Michael," she gasped. A sudden weakness deadened her muscles, and she found herself panting for breath. "I didn't see you..." She lifted a trembling finger and pointed over the wall. "The shifters, I have them on the run, I—"

"The shifters are finished, child. The battle is over." His voice was steady, but a look of extreme caution lit the backs of his eyes as he offered a hand. "Come. Let's find your friends."

Everything he was saying made sense. Every impulse she had was to follow. But some uncertain emotion made her hold back. Made her look at the hand as if it was the enemy, not the gentle offering of a friend.

"I..." She held back, completely unaware that the heels of her shoes were just inches from the edge of the wall. "I don't..."

A sudden voice called her to attention. Echoing up over the scorched stones. He was frantic but determined. And very, very much alive.

"Dylan!" She was off like a shot. Leaving Michael standing on the ledge behind her. Leaving the smoldering remains of the battlefield smoking in her wake. Her feet couldn't seem to move fast enough as they flew down the crooked steps, and by the time she reached the courtyard her eyes were swimming with a sea of unshed tears.

There he was. Standing amidst the chaos. A curl of smoke still rising from his arms. In the flurry of chaos that had taken over the monastery, he was the only thing standing still.

The second their eyes met they came together. She ran without thinking into his outstretched arms. It seemed silly now, that she'd thought something like words could come between them. That anything in the world could hold them back.

She buried her face in his jacket as his hands came up over her head. They tangled in her long hair, anchoring her close as his chest fell up and down with silent, jerking breaths. His skin was hot to the touch, flushed from the flames still writhing on the battlefield, and when Katerina finally pulled back her cheek was wet with blood. She lifted an uncertain hand.

"Are you...are you okay?"

Her eyes roved frantically over his body, searching for a wound, but whatever had happened he didn't seem aware of it himself. His eyes were fixed solely on her face. And for one of the first times since they'd met, she couldn't begin to interpret his expression.

"I'm fine," he said slowly. There was a pause, during which his eyes flickered surreptitiously down to her hands before locking onto her once more. "...what about you?"

It's caution, she realized. *That's what his emotion is. The same caution as Michael.*

She wanted to reassure him. Wanted to tell him that everything was going to be okay. That she'd only used her devastating power to save his life. That she was still the same person.

But all those words fell short.

Instead, she simply stared at him. Too overwhelmed to speak. Too tired to stand. Too scared to do anything other than linger in his arms, praying that terrible caution would go away.

He took one look at her face and nodded shortly. More to himself than to her.

"Come on," he said quietly, leading her quickly away from the ever-growing throng of people.

KATERINA MAY HAVE SPENT the last two weeks living in the monastery but her days were strictly planned out, and she'd followed a very specific route. There were still places she'd never gone before. The little garden, blossoming behind the sanctuary wall, for example. It was brand new.

"Who the hell are you?"

The princess tore her eyes away from the delicate blossoms and stared at Dylan with abject fear. He had waited until they were completely alone to ask the question. Waited until they were safe from the gaze of probing eyes. But now that they were, he couldn't hold it in a second longer.

"*Katerina.*" He took her by the shoulders, staring deep into her eyes. "Who are you?"

At this point, she should have been grateful that he didn't ask *what* she was. After her little fire display, he would certainly have been entitled. However, despite the validity of his question, a spark of anger burned in her chest. *He* wanted answers, did he? Well, join the freakin' club.

"Who am *I*?" she repeated, just barely holding on to her temper. "Who the hell are YOU?"

A flash of uncertainly danced through his eyes, but it was quickly overshadowed by that habitual anger. The anger he wore as a cloak to ward off such unwelcome intrusions.

"You really think this is the time—"

"This is *exactly* the time!" she shouted, shaking from head to toe. She didn't know the answer to his question, but that wasn't going to stop her from asking hers. The time had come to put all their cards on the table. They'd held these secrets long enough.

Dylan stood in front of her, not moving, not offering anything.

"Why did the fairies send me to you?" she demanded, firing each question like an arrow, pointed straight at his heart. "Why do you happen to know the names and lineage of every duke and earl in the kingdom? Why was Cassiel worried I had specifically sought *you* out, when we first met?"

Dylan paled a little more with each question, retreating into himself. "Katerina, I don't—"

"You cannot hold a person responsible for the sins of their family." She quoted the exact words he'd said to her that day at the glen. The day she'd told him her real name. "If anyone knows that, it's me."

It fell between them like an accusation, burning hard and true.

"What does that mean?" she insisted. "Who are you, Dylan? No lies—tell me the *truth*!"

"The *truth*—" He pulled away suddenly, shivering like a little boy. Eyes huge and uncertain. Breath coming in broken gasps. A wave of absolute fear washed over him, then left, leaving him perfectly still. "The truth is that you're not the only royal on the run."

Chapter 14

"My name is Dylan Hale."

The princess and the ranger sat on a bench in the garden. The uproar following the fiery end to the supply run was still raging, but in their little part of the monastery things were quiet.

Dylan was shaken, yet strangely calm.

He'd held out for as long as he could. Counted on that infallible strength to save him. Prayed for a miracle that would allow him to walk away. But his time had run out. When he finally spoke that impenetrable shield was gone, and he was unexpectedly quiet.

"I'm the only son of Aldrich Hale. Crown prince of Belaria."

Katerina pulled in a quick gasp but maintained a carefully neutral expression.

Belaria was the cautionary tale. A once-prosperous kingdom which ignored the cries of people begging for reform. A once-prosperous kingdom destroyed in a grisly, violent revolution. Katerina remembered hearing her father talk about it when she was younger. Hearing him lament the royal family and plot with his council as to how best to help their cause. It was one of the only times in her life she had seen him express any kind of solidarity or compassion.

"You made it out before..." She trailed off at the look on his face, feeling as though she'd been dunked in cold water. "I mean...you made it out?"

Dylan bowed his head, eyes fixed on a thin crack spider-webbing up the stone tiles. "I grew up knowing that the people hated my family. I was too young to understand why, and the palace has a way of shielding you from such things. But that tension was always there. When I got older, saw the things they were doing, the people they really were...I started to hate them, too."

The air was thick and warm, but he shivered. He couldn't seem to stop.

"When I was fourteen, I ran away. I didn't want to be part of the oppression I saw going on around me—part of the system." He paused for a moment, like he wished the story ended there, before continuing in that same quiet voice. "A week after I left, I heard the news. There had been an uprising. The entire royal family had been slaughtered."

Katerina held her tongue, but her control ended there. Silent tears poured down her face as she reached out to take his hand. Crying where he could not. Showing heartache and feeling, while his face was like cold stone. He glanced down at their intertwined fingers, then back up at the tower.

"The fairies found me. Half-dead. Brought me here. Told me to wait out the storm. For six months, that's what I did. Six months and it just about killed me."

Literally.

Katerina pictured a little boy sitting on the high stone ledge. Gazing out over the mountains beyond. A boy without a family. A king without a throne. So lost and broken and alone that the only thing he could think to do...was jump.

"Michael urged me to go back," he said suddenly. "To take the throne and rule in a different way than the rest of my family. To rule for good. The people didn't hold their sins against me—I would be welcomed back with open arms. But I...I couldn't do it." He took a deep breath and pulled his hand away. Suddenly ready to be finished with the story. Suddenly ready to rush to the end. "I became a ranger instead. Changed my name, my accent. Did everything I could to get lost in the world. I was lost so long that everyone stopped looking." He suddenly lifted his head and turned to Katerina. "Until a few years later...I met you."

The princess sat numb on the bench, trying to absorb everything she'd just heard. In a strange way, it made perfect sense. In a strange way, it was like a part of her had always expected it.

The first thing she'd noticed about Dylan was the way he stood out. Even in the grimy tavern, half-drunk and fighting off vampires, it was clear the man was something more. He might have changed his name, dropped his accent, but there were things about him that no amount of time could ever erase. It was a quality; that's what the people back home always used to call it. A royal quality that one could neither gain nor lose. You either had it or you didn't. It was in your blood.

Dylan's grace and charm, the way he clipped certain vowels, his inexplicable knowledge of the world, right down to the way he held a wine glass. She should have known. Maybe she did.

"When Marigold sent me to find you," she said softly, peering up hesitantly, "she said I needed to be with someone who could keep me safe. Someone who had done this sort of thing before..."

Dylan laughed shortly, dark hair swinging into his eyes. "Real subtle, fairies are." The hint of a smile lingered in his eyes as he shook his head. "A runaway prince and an exiled princess. I'm sure she found a poetic kind of symmetry in that."

Katerina smiled back. Even wider when she imagined her own experience, but with a fourteen-year-old Dylan instead. Choking down Marigold's tonics. Fighting off Nixie when she tried to braid his hair. But the smile faded as another quiet truth clicked suddenly into place. "That night in Vale..."

Dylan bowed his head with a sigh. It was a night he'd clearly gone back to many times, she realized. "How could we be together? Tell me. How?" Those blue eyes tightened with unspeakable pain as they found hers. "Because I can't see it. You want, more than anything, to return to your castle and take your place on the throne. I want, more than anything, to stay away. How could we be together? A princess whose crown has been stolen and a prince who's spent his entire life trying to bury his own crown."

Katerina felt like she'd been hit in the face. Like some icy hand had twisted the knife. But, at the same time, a slow smile crept up her cheeks. Finally—*at last*—it all made sense! Every strange gesture, every fleeting look she didn't understand. A thousand secrets and deflections. A thousand misdirections and nights lost to over-analyzing his every move. It all finally made sense!

"...are you smiling?"

The smile froze as Katerina looked up with a start. "What? No. No."

"You are!" He was enraged. "I can't believe it! You actually are!"

She tried to get it under control, to no avail. "No, I swear I'm not. I just—"

"You finally get what you want. I finally break down and tell you all those answers you've been dying to hear, and you sit there grinning like some Carpathian chimp!"

"Because of *you*!" she exclaimed, throwing up her hands. "Why couldn't you have just told me all that from the beginning? Why keep it a secret—"

"Oh, I don't know," he shouted back, "maybe because I'm bloody in love with you!"

There was a moment of silence.

Well, that's one way to say it...

The words echoed between them as the heated back and forth ended abruptly. It was quiet for a few seconds before Dylan finally broke it, his eyes locked safely on the ground. "I'm in love with you...but the only thing I know for certain is that the two of us can't be together." The words seemed to rip out of him, tearing off pieces as they went. However, no matter what the cost, his voice was firm. "Why would I tell you? Why wouldn't I have tried to stay away?"

Katerina understood what he was saying, but it wasn't as simple as all that. And it certainly wasn't a decision he could make for her. Not that he'd exactly risen to the occasion. Her eyes sparked as half a dozen stolen kisses flashed through her mind. "Oh, and a fine job you did staying away."

His head jerked up as his eyes burned with accusation. "Well, it's not like you make it easy! Falling off cliffs, getting attacked in the woods, looking up at me with those big dreamy eyes? You're lucky it wasn't worse!"

"*Worse?!*" Her eyebrows arched in astonishment. "Think about what you're saying!"

He let out his breath with a frustrated sigh. "I know, and I'm sorry. I don't mean it like that; it's just—"

"No. It's just nothing!" She pushed to her feet, unable to sit a moment longer. "It's all well and good for you to keep your little secret, Dylan. For you to keep your reasons to yourself. But *I* was the one left out in the cold! *I* was the one who said that I love you, then watched you throw it back in my face! Me, not you! *I'm* the one who suffered all the consequences of *your* decision!"

"You think I haven't suffered?" He pushed to his feet as well, towering over her from just inches away. "You think this has been fun for me? Sleeping beside you *every night*, knowing I can never have you? Walking beside you *every day*, watching us grow a little further apart? You have no idea how many times I almost told you. How many times I almost—"

"Then why didn't you?!" She grabbed the front of his jacket, trying to shake the answer right out of him. Another smear of blood stained the tops of her knuckles, but she was too upset to notice it. "Why didn't you just tell me the truth—"

"Because it would be over then!"

The garden fell deathly quiet as his face crumpled in pain.

"It would be over," he said again, softer this time, "and any chance we had would be—"

She didn't think. She kissed him. A kiss that put all others to shame.

His eyes flew open in surprise as she locked her wrists behind his neck, pulling him down so she could reach. He closed them and pulled her up instead, lifting her effortlessly off the ground as his arms circled around her back with a force that threatened to crush her.

He loves me. I don't care what else he said...he said that he loves me.

A radiant smile flushed her face as the kiss deepened and their bodies melded into one. Her skin tingled with sparks of electricity. Her blood flew hot through her veins, heating her fingers as they twisted into his hair. It was too much, and not enough all at the same time. Her heart was pounding, her head was spinning. It was so overwhelming she thought she might faint—

"*Ow.*"

Cold air rushed between them as Dylan pulled back sharply, staring down at his chest. The princess' face paled as she quickly hid her hands behind her back.

"I'm sorry," she apologized immediately. "Did I burn you? I'm so sorry."

"No, it's..." He reached into his shirt and pulled out her mother's pendant. It was glowing as fiercely as she'd ever seen. She could feel the heat from where she stood. "It's this." He gingerly held it away from his body, fingers wrapped around the chain. "Has it ever done that before?"

"No. Never." Katerina reached for the stone with a frown, holding it lightly in the palm of her hand. It may have burned him, but to her it felt as natural as could be. "Maybe it's on the fritz or something. Got smashed when you were running up the..." She trailed off when she realized that he was looking not at the pendant, but at her own hands. Hands he had seen do so much damage. Hands that had recently been wrapped in his hair.

"Katerina—"

"I don't know what I am." She answered the question before he could ask it, lowering those hands slowly to her side. "That's the truth, I promise." She tentatively lifted her gaze to his, searching for any kind of hope. "But I think...I think that I'm something like you."

He hesitated a moment, weighing his options, then his lips twitched up in a smile. "Well, *I'm* delighted." His finger slipped beneath her chin, tilting up her face as he leaned down for another kiss. "There are worse things to be..."

That's when the first flaming arrow fired over the gate.

Chapter 15

"DYLAN!"

They heard the shouting before they even made it out of the garden. Before they'd taken a sudden step back, staring down in unison at a rose bush that had burst into flames.

Their heads snapped up at the same time. Then they started running.

In one corridor and out another. Pushing past people, who were just as frantically pushing past them. Katerina was vaguely aware that they seemed to be moving against the tide, but at this point it hardly mattered. The courtyard was where the action was happening. The courtyard was where the screaming had started. It was also where they'd left their friends.

"DYLAN!" They heard it again the moment they stepped outside. "KAT!"

Cassiel and Tanya were standing in the middle of the terrace, the only people not moving in a sea of blurred faces. Behind them, the outer wall of the monastery had caught fire. Some people were trying to put it out, while others were taking cover from the swarm of flying arrows. At the moment, however, neither problem was their immediate concern.

"Dylan!" Cassiel yelled again, in confirmation this time. He darted swiftly through the crowd, dragging Tanya along with him. "You're all right?"

The two men shared a silent look, and the question was compartmentalized for another time. In the meanwhile, the fae nodded swiftly and cocked his head to the wall.

"We've got a problem."

It seemed the castle's best archers had finally arrived. Not only were they able to hit the outside of the monastery, but their lethal arrows were flying over the top of the wall. A problem all by itself, only these arrows were covered in—

"...flames," Katerina whispered.

The four friends watched in silent horror as the pile of cedar logs for rebuilding the bridge caught fire. A moment later, the curtains inside the dining hall started to burn.

"Yep. Seems someone gave them the idea." Tanya jerked her head instinctively as a flaming arrow whizzed past her cheek. "You can end a battle quickly if you just set your enemies on fire."

The princess glanced over nervously, but Tanya flashed her a grin. On her other side, Cassiel was harder to read. But he gave the princess a hand up as she and Dylan joined them on the ledge.

Sure enough, it looked like the entire royal army was aflame. Their swarm of red and black uniforms had vanished completely under a smoky cloud. A cloud that was steadily growing bigger and closer as volley after volley of fire-tipped arrows headed their way.

"We're not going to win this," Katerina murmured, realizing the truth in the words the second they passed her lips. "All of us, all these people...are going to lose."

Dylan set his jaw, glaring viciously over the high walls. "Not if I can help it."

A second later, he leapt back down into the courtyard. Joining the dwindling group of people racing buckets from the well to those areas most affected by the fire. Many areas had already been given up on—engulfed in the burning flames. Faster and faster they ran. Little buckets of water, spilling drops onto the tile. It would not be enough. It would not be nearly enough.

"Cass, get down here and help!"

The fae stepped forward automatically to heed Dylan's call, but paused as he looked out over the desperate scene. One look at the grim line of his mouth, and Katerina knew she was right.

This fight was already over. As long as the arrows kept coming, they were going to lose.

She thought of the villagers she'd come to know since her arrival. Grinelda, down in the kitchens. The lisping bartender who ran the tavern. She thought of the finger-paintings and all those children who came to this place seeking refuge. Rose was fighting her way towards them through the fire. In the background, she thought she saw Michael standing in the smoke.

I can't let it happen. No matter what, Talsing Sanctuary cannot fall.

Just like that, it was decided. It was as though a power greater than herself had taken over. It guided her movements. Squaring her shoulders. Steadying her step. Her eyes flickered to the faces around her—the best faces she knew. She bid them all a silent goodbye, edging her way backwards up to the little ledge. The one where Dylan had sat as a child, staring over the endless peaks.

His was the last face she saw. Smeared with soot and blood. Calling out some desperate order she couldn't seem to hear over the ringing in her ears. A fleeting smile passed over her face as she stared at him. Immortalizing it forever. Then she turned her back and climbed onto the ledge.

It wasn't done with any fanfare. It wasn't done as anything more than a simple necessity. An answer to a question. A quiet solution to save their lives. The princess stepped to the very edge of the wall and gazed over the cliff. It was what she had to offer. The only sacrifice she could make.

"KATERINA!"

She half-turned to look over her shoulder. A part of her shouldn't have been surprised. A gust of wind swept through the cloud of smoke, and for a split second she saw Dylan standing there. For a split second, the two of them locked eyes.

He was terrified. There was no other word to describe it. And not for himself, although he was at the top of the army's most-wanted list. Not even for the people of Talsing, who were all about to lose their lives. He was focused on one life. On a certain girl he would have given his own life a million times over to save.

He didn't say a word. He just shook his head. Staring with wide eyes through the smoke.

Don't. Please.

It was written all over his face, clear as day.

The princess smiled and pressed her fingers to her lips. Then to her heart. Then, before she could talk herself out of it, she turned back towards the cliff. Another gust of wind swelled up around them, tangling her hair as she stared into the abyss. She said a silent prayer, a silent farewell.

Then she took a breath...and jumped.

You don't get to choose your stars.

Katerina's mother had told her that once. She was only a little girl, sitting on the queen's lap as she played with the royal pendant. Batting it back and forth.

Delighting in the shards of ruby-tinted light that danced along the wall. Adelaide smiled at her daughter and said the words again.

You don't get to choose your stars. But there is a reason those stars chose you.

The princess never understood the meaning of those words until that very moment.

...there is a reason those stars chose you.

A girl jumped over the cliff that day.

A DRAGON FLEW UP IN her place.

It was a feeling unlike any other. A sudden mending of what Katerina didn't know had been broken. A sudden completion of what she hadn't realized she'd been without.

A sense of belonging. Calming that aching storm within her heart.

There were distant shouts and cries from both sides as she flapped her powerful wings, feeling the air rush up beneath them as she took to the skies.

Her muscles, so slender and weak as a human, stretched out strong and lean. Her skin had shed its smooth ivory and was covered in a thick armor of ruby scales. Her piercing eyes roved over the mountains, trying to decide what to do with it. With the raging fire that was building up inside.

If I let the army live, they'll burn the monastery to the ground. Killing everyone inside. If I let the army live, they'll never stop coming. They'll never stop fighting. Everyone I've ever loved will be lost.

The world tilted sharply to the side as she angled her body around for another pass. From so high up, the soldiers looked like little figurines. The kinds of toys that she and Kailas used to play with as children. They looked much different up close. They looked angry. And afraid. *Very* afraid.

In the end, she had to close her eyes. She knew it had to happen, but she couldn't make herself watch. It didn't matter. Eyes closed or open, her body seemed to know what to do.

A shower of arrows ricocheted harmlessly off her shining neck as she glided low along the frosty embankment. The first time, nothing happened. The second time, she let loose a deafening roar and a wave of deadly fire spewed from her mouth.

The tents went up in flames. The people were soon to follow. An entire battalion, destroyed in less than a minute. Those who were able ran for the trees. Those who had more sense tried to take cover. They were few and far between. There was no escaping a dragon's fire. It sought you out like it had a mind of its own. Bringing a swift and brutal justice to everyone in its path.

Smoke curled in the air and remnants of the fire danced in her eyes as Katerina left the burning army behind her and circled back over the ravine. Freed from the constant onslaught of arrows, the people of Talsing had been able to get the fires mostly under control. The monastery was saved, at least for now, but it wouldn't be enough to change her mind.

As long as she stayed there, the place would always be in danger. As long as she and her friends remained, the entire sanctuary would live under constant threat.

It was something she could no longer allow.

She came down as lightly as she could. Perched upon the landing where she and her friends used to stand watch. Taloned claws gripped the edge of the crenulated stone as she lifted her head and waited, staring calmly at the mass of shell-shocked people scattering in her wake.

Slowly, very slowly, three tentative faces ventured out from the crowd. They were followed by a fourth. One that surprised Katerina but seemed to fit at the same time.

Together, Tanya, Cassiel, Dylan, and Rose made their way towards her. Moving as one would when approaching a wild animal. Their eyes bright with wonder and fear.

"Is it really her?" Tanya whispered, staring incredulously at the long, whipping tail.

Katerina bowed her head as Dylan took a step forward and nodded.

"It's her."

He alone was looking at her without a trace of fear. He was shocked, astonished, bewildered, uncertain, and a whole host of other things. But afraid...he was not.

"Something like me?" He cocked an eyebrow and ran a tentative hand along the smooth curve of her neck. "I'm afraid you have massively overestimated me, Your Highness."

He and Katerina shared a secret smile as the rest of them anxiously hovered behind.

"I say we stab it. Just to be sure." The others turned to Cassiel in disbelief and he shrugged defensively, his hand on his blade. "What? It's a bloomin' dragon! A nightmarish beast! If it's really Katerina, then she won't kill us when we're through."

Wanna bet?

Two curls of smoke rose threateningly from her nostrils as Dylan glanced back with a grin.

"No one's stabbing anyone. But if I'm not mistaken...we're leaving?" He phrased it as a question and turned back to search her eyes.

She nodded slowly, lowered a wing, then cocked her head with a fiery grin toward the horizon.

Tanya lifted her eyebrows, and even the all-confident Rose took a step back. "Wait. She wants us to..."

"No," Cassiel shook his head firmly. "Absolutely not."

Dylan turned around again, keeping one hand on Katerina at the same time. "Come on, you little coward. You know she's right. We can't stay here anymore. It's time to leave."

The fae took a step back, the face of a dragon reflected fearfully in his dark eyes. "Not in a million freakin' years," he murmured, backing away another step. He wasn't entirely sure that his friend was buried beneath those scales. And even if she was, he wasn't entirely sure it would matter. "I do a lot of things for you, Dylan, but that's too much."

"Oh, come on," Tanya teased, stepping up onto Katerina's steady wing. "You're not going to let me go by myself, are you? What if she decides to eat me along the way?"

Cassiel lifted a hand to stop her, literally frozen with indecision, before he took a deep breath and reluctantly followed suit. "I have a bad feeling about this..."

Katerina blew a cloud of smoke at him, and he kicked out with his foot. "Stop that! Bad dragon!"

Rose was close behind, eyeing the princess with a look of extreme caution. "So, you and me...we're cool, right? That whole apology bit worked?"

Katerina snickered—as well as a dragon can snicker—and stooped closer to the ground so the shifter would have an easier time climbing up. She did so nervously, and settled at Tanya's side.

In the end, the only person left was Dylan. The only person who required no invitation.

With the slightly manic grin of an adrenaline junky whose greatest fantasy had just come to life, he sprang lightly onto her back and settled down—the wind in his hair, the horizon in his eyes. "So, where to, princess?"

Good question.

One powerful beat of her wings, and the monastery vanished beneath him. Disappearing into the misty haze as she turned her eyes towards the sunset and took flight.

Where to? She wasn't sure.

But, for possibly the first time in her entire life, she wasn't afraid to find out.

THE END

Evermore

Evermore Blurb

She will fight for what is hers.

When Katerina unlocks her secret power and sets the entire royal army ablaze, the stakes to an already dangerous game soar even higher. As her brother gathers his bannermen to destroy her once and for all, the princess must appeal to the people themselves.

And not just the people. If she wants to take back the throne, she'll need the entire supernatural community by her side.

In a race against time, Katerina and her friends scour the countryside. Forging new alliances and making new enemies at the same time. Their path is dangerous enough, without the dark wizard working against them, and Katerina soon discovers that things aren't always as they seem.

Can the princess rally the support of her people? Can she reconcile the girl she once was, with the queen she must become? With all the odds stacked against her...

...can she ever take back the throne?

The Queen's Alpha Series

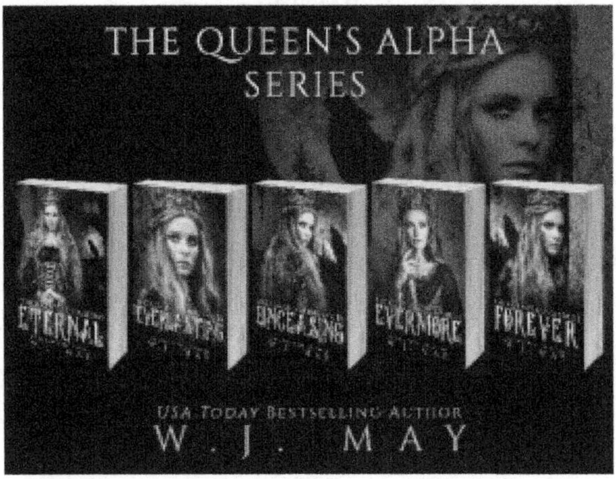

Eternal
Everlasting
Unceasing
Evermore
Forever

Find W.J. May

Website:
http://www.wanitamay.yolasite.com
Facebook:
https://www.facebook.com/pages/Author-WJ-May-FAN-PAGE/141170442608149
Newsletter:
SIGN UP FOR W.J. May's Newsletter to find out about new releases, updates, cover reveals and even freebies!
http://eepurl.com/97aYf

USA TODAY
BESTSELLING AUTHOR
W.J. MAY
bring fantasy to life...

More books by W.J. May

The Chronicles of Kerrigan

Book I - *Rae of Hope* is FREE!
Book Trailer
http://www.youtube.com/watch?v=gILAwXxx8MU
Book II - *Dark Nebula*
Book Trailer:
http://www.youtube.com/watch?v=Ca24STi_bFM
Book III - *House of Cards*
Book IV - *Royal Tea*
Book V - *Under Fire*
Book VI - *End in Sight*
Book VII – *Hidden Darkness*
Book VIII – *Twisted Together*
Book IX – *Mark of Fate*
Book X – *Strength & Power*
Book XI – *Last One Standing*
BOOK XII – *Rae of Light*

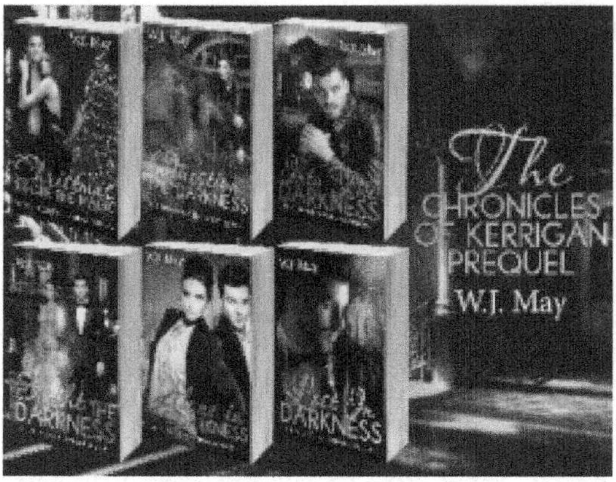

PREQUEL –

- Christmas Before the Magic
- Question the Darkness
- Into the Darkness
- Fight the Darkness
- Alone the Darkness
- Lost the Darkness

SEQUEL –

- Matter of Time
- Time Piece
- Second Chance
- Glitch in Time
- Our Time
- Precious Time

Hidden Secrets Saga:

Download Seventh Mark part 1 For FREE

Book Trailer:

http://www.youtube.com/watch?v=Y-_vVYC1gvo

Like most teenagers, Rouge is trying to figure out who she is and what she wants to be. With little knowledge about her past, she has questions but has never tried to find the answers. Everything changes when she befriends a strangely intoxicating family. Siblings Grace and Michael, appear to have secrets which seem connected to Rouge. Her hunch is confirmed when a horrible incident occurs at an outdoor party. Rouge may be the only one who can find the answer.

An ancient journal, a Sioghra necklace and a special mark force life-altering decisions for a girl who grew up unprepared to fight for her life or others.

All secrets have a cost and Rouge's determination to find the truth can only lead to trouble...or something even more sinister.

RADIUM HALOS - THE SENSELESS SERIES

Book 1 is FREE:

Everyone needs to be a hero at one point in their life.

The small town of Elliot Lake will never be the same again.

Caught in a sudden thunderstorm, Zoe, a high school senior from Elliot Lake, and five of her friends take shelter in an abandoned uranium mine. Over the next few days, Zoe's hearing sharpens drastically, beyond what any normal human being can detect. She tells her friends, only to learn that four others have an increased sense as well. Only Kieran, the new boy from Scotland, isn't affected.

Fashioning themselves into superheroes, the group tries to stop the strange occurrences happening in their little town. Muggings, break-ins, disappearances, and murder begin to hit too close to home. It leads the team to think someone knows about their secret - someone who wants them all dead.

An incredulous group of heroes. A traitor in the midst. Some dreams are written in blood.

Courage Runs Red
The Blood Red Series
Book 1 is FREE

WHAT IF COURAGE WAS your only option?

When Kallie lands a college interview with the city's new hot-shot police officer, she has no idea everything in her life is about to change. The detective is young, handsome and seems to have an unnatural ability to stop the increasing local crime rate. Detective Liam's particular interest in Kallie sends her heart and head stumbling over each other.

When a raging blood feud between vampires spills into her home, Kallie gets caught in the middle. Torn between love and family loyalty she must find the courage to fight what she fears the most and possibly risk everything, even if it means dying for those she loves.

Daughter of Darkness

VICTORIA

Only Death Could Stop Her Now

The Daughters of Darkness is a series of female heroines who may or may not know each other, but all have the same father, Vlad Montour.

Victoria is a Hunter Vampire

HUNTRESS SERIES
USA TODAY BESTSELLING AUTHOR
W.J. MAY
LOOK BACK
MASTER
PERMISSION

PROPHECY SERIES
USA TODAY BESTSELLING AUTHOR
• W.J. MAY •
PROPHECY
• W.J. MAY •
PROPHECY
• W.J. MAY •
PROPHECY
• W.J. MAY •

The Chronicles of
KERRIGAN
W.J. May
RAE OF HOPE
DARK NEBULA
HOUSE OF CARDS
ROYAL TEA
UNDER FIRE
END IN SIGHT
W.J. May
Chronicles of
KERRIGAN

THE HIDDEN
SECRETS SAGA
W.J. MAY
COMPELLED
CHOSEN THREE
THE HIDDEN
SECRETS SAGA

Don't miss out!

Click the button below and you can sign up to receive emails whenever W.J. May publishes a new book. There's no charge and no obligation.

https://books2read.com/r/B-A-SSF-FGDR

BOOKS 2 READ

Connecting independent readers to independent writers.

Did you love *Unceasing*? Then you should read *The Chronicles of Kerrigan Box Set Books # 1 - 6* by W.J. May!

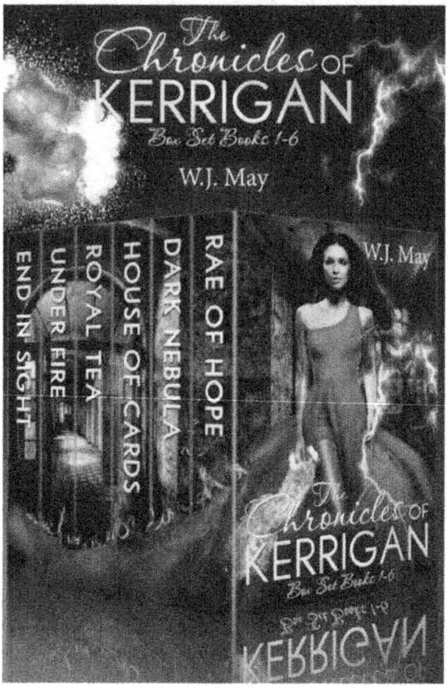

Join Rae Kerrigan & start an amazing adventure! By USA Today Bestseller WJ May

The Chronicles of Kerrigan BoxSet

Bk 1 - Rae of Hope

How hard do you have to shake the family tree to find the truth about the past?

15 yr-old Rae Kerrigan never knew her family's history. Her mother & father died when she was young and it's only when she accepts a scholarship to the prestigious Guilder Boarding School in England that a mysterious family secret is revealed.

Will the sins of the father be the sins of the daughter?

As Rae struggles with new friends, a new school & a star-struck forbidden love, she must also face the ultimate challenge: receive a tattoo on her 16th birthday with specific powers that may bind her to an unspeakable darkness. It's up to Rae to undo the darkness in her family's past and have a ray of hope for her future.

Bk 2 - Dark Nebula

Nothing is as it seems anymore.

Leery from the horrifying incident at the end of her first year at Guilder, Rae's determined to learn more about her new tattoo. Her expectations are high, but all hopes of happiness turn into shattered dreams the moment she steps back on campus.

Lies & secrets are everywhere, and a betrayal cuts Rae deeply. Among her conflicts & enemies, it appears her father is reaching out from beyond the grave to ruin her life. With no one to trust, Rae doesn't know who to turn to for help.

Has her destiny been written? Or will she become the one thing she hates the most-her father's prodigy.

Bk 3 - House of Cards

Rae Kerrigan is 3months away from graduating from Guilder. She's now moonlighting as an operative for the Privy Council, a black ops division for British Intelligence. She's given a mentor, Jennifer, who fights like a demon.Rae finds a strange maternal bond with her. At the same time, she finds a new friend when Devon disappoints her once again.

When the Privy Council ask for her help, she finds a friend, and a link, to the Xavier Knights–another agency similar to the PCs.

Will she lose herself in the confusions of the past and present? What will it mean for her future?

Book 4 - Royal Tea

The Queen of England has requested the help of the Privy Council. Someone is trying to kill her son's fiancé. The HRH Prince plans to marry a commoner, and his bride has a secret no one knows but the Privy Council. She has a tatù. When the Privy Council turns to Rae for help, she can't possibly say no; not even when they make Devon her partner for this assignment.

Rae would rather be anywhere but with Devon, especially since she believes her mother to be alive, despite the Privy Council's assurances to the contrary. How can Rae find proof of life for her mother, come to terms with her feelings for Devon, and manage to save the Princess, all while dressed for tea?

When the enigma, the secrets and the skeletons in the closet begin to be exposed, can Rae handle the truth?

Book 5 - Under Fire

Rae Kerrigan is determined to find her mother. No amount of convincing from

Devon, or the Privy Council, is going to make her believe her mother is not alive, and Rae will stop at nothing to find her.
Torn between friendship and loyalty, Rae must also choose between Luke and Devon. She can't continue to deny, or fool herself, any longer. The heart wants what the heart wants.

Book 6 - End in Sight

When life couldn't get anymore confusing, fate steps in and throws a curveball.

Also by W.J. May

Bit-Lit Series
Lost Vampire
Cost of Blood
Price of Death

Blood Red Series
Courage Runs Red
The Night Watch
Marked by Courage
Forever Night

Daughters of Darkness: Victoria's Journey
Victoria
Huntress
Coveted (A Vampire & Paranormal Romance)
Twisted

Hidden Secrets Saga
Seventh Mark - Part 1
Seventh Mark - Part 2
Marked By Destiny

Compelled
Fate's Intervention
Chosen Three
The Hidden Secrets Saga: The Complete Series

Paranormal Huntress Series
Never Look Back
Coven Master
Alpha's Permission

Prophecy Series
Only the Beginning
White Winter
Secrets of Destiny

The Chronicles of Kerrigan
Rae of Hope
Dark Nebula
House of Cards
Royal Tea
Under Fire
End in Sight
Hidden Darkness
Twisted Together
Mark of Fate
Strength & Power
Last One Standing
Rae of Light
The Chronicles of Kerrigan Box Set Books # 1 - 6

The Chronicles of Kerrigan: Gabriel

Living in the Past

Staring at the Future

Present For Today

The Chronicles of Kerrigan Prequel

Question the Darkness

Into the Darkness

Fight the Darkness

Alone in the Darkness

Lost in Darkness

Christmas Before the Magic

The Chronicles of Kerrigan Prequel Series Books #1-3

The Chronicles of Kerrigan Sequel

A Matter of Time

Time Piece

Second Chance

Glitch in Time

Our Time

Precious Time

The Hidden Secrets Saga

Seventh Mark (part 1 & 2)

The Queen's Alpha Series

Eternal

Everlasting
Unceasing
Evermore

The Senseless Series
Radium Halos
Radium Halos - Part 2
Nonsense

Standalone
Shadow of Doubt (Part 1 & 2)
Five Shades of Fantasy
Shadow of Doubt - Part 1
Shadow of Doubt - Part 2
Four and a Half Shades of Fantasy
Dream Fighter
What Creeps in the Night
Forest of the Forbidden
Arcane Forest: A Fantasy Anthology
Ancient Blood of the Vampire and Werewolf

Made in the USA
Monee, IL
16 October 2020

45257930R00105